the perfect smile

(a jessie hunt psychological suspense—book 4)

blake pierce

Blake Pierce

Blake Pierce is author of the bestselling RILEY PAGE mystery series, which includes fifteen books (and counting). Blake Pierce is also the author of the MACKENZIE WHITE mystery series, comprising thirteen books (and counting); of the AVERY BLACK mystery series, comprising six books; of the KERI LOCKE mystery series, comprising five books; of the MAKING OF RILEY PAIGE mystery series, comprising five books (and counting); of the KATE WISE mystery series, comprising six books (and counting); of the CHLOE FINE psychological suspense mystery, comprising six books (and counting); and of the JESSE HUNT psychological suspense thriller series, comprising five books (and counting).

An avid reader and lifelong fan of the mystery and thriller genres, Blake loves to hear from you, so please feel free to visit www.blakepierceauthor.com to learn more and stay in touch.

BOOKS BY BLAKE PIERCE

A JESSIE HUNT PSYCHOLOGICAL SUSPENSE SERIES
THE PERFECT WIFE (Book #1)
THE PERFECT BLOCK (Book #2)
THE PERFECT HOUSE (Book #3)
THE PERFECT SMILE (Book #4)
THE PERFECT LIE (Book #5)

CHLOE FINE PSYCHOLOGICAL SUSPENSE SERIES
NEXT DOOR (Book #1)
A NEIGHBOR'S LIE (Book #2)
CUL DE SAC (Book #3)
SILENT NEIGHBOR (Book #4)
HOMECOMING (Book #5)
TINTED WINDOWS (Book #6)

KATE WISE MYSTERY SERIES
IF SHE KNEW (Book #1)
IF SHE SAW (Book #2)
IF SHE RAN (Book #3)
IF SHE HID (Book #4)
IF SHE FLED (Book #5)
IF SHE FEARED (Book #6)

THE MAKING OF RILEY PAIGE SERIES
WATCHING (Book #1)
WAITING (Book #2)
LURING (Book #3)
TAKING (Book #4)
STALKING (Book #5)

RILEY PAIGE MYSTERY SERIES
ONCE GONE (Book #1)
ONCE TAKEN (Book #2)
ONCE CRAVED (Book #3)
ONCE LURED (Book #4)
ONCE HUNTED (Book #5)
ONCE PINED (Book #6)
ONCE FORSAKEN (Book #7)
ONCE COLD (Book #8)
ONCE STALKED (Book #9)
ONCE LOST (Book #10)
ONCE BURIED (Book #11)
ONCE BOUND (Book #12)

PROLOGUE

When Gabrielle got back to her two-bedroom rented house in Studio City, it was almost five in the afternoon. She'd spent most of the day at the beach with a guy she'd been seeing. It was fun—her date had rented a cabana at the Annenberg Beach House in Santa Monica and the food and adult beverages were kept constantly flowing.

But now she felt crispy from the sun and slightly uncomfortable from the endless snacking. She knew she couldn't have too many afternoons like that if she wanted to keep her body in the kind of shape that made other guys pretend not to stare when she sashayed by.

As she opened the glass front door of the house, she admired her reflection. She might have felt bloated but she still looked great. Her long dark hair had a windswept quality from the continuous ocean breeze. Her deeply tanned skin might be smarting but at least it was glowing. And in her platform sandals, she topped out at well over six feet tall.

When she got inside the house, she could immediately hear Claire, her friend and housemate, engaged in a heated phone conversation. She made a token attempt to ignore what was being said before giving in to curiosity.

"We can't see each other anymore," she heard Claire say and then pause for the inevitable negative reaction. After a few seconds of silence, she responded to whatever the other person had said.

"It's just not a fit," Claire replied calmly, with a firm but apologetic tone. "It would be best for both of us to simply move on."

Gabrielle smiled to herself. She was pretty adept at these kinds of breakup calls. But Claire was an expert. She always managed to let the guy down easy, making him think that it was her insecurities and not the greener grass of the next guy that was the issue.

But this time, it sounded like the process was a bit bumpier. Claire's soon-to-be-ex was slightly audible, even multiple rooms away. After what sounded like a tirade during which her housemate remained silent, Claire finally responded in a quiet but forceful voice.

"I'm sorry you feel that way," she said. "But this can't come as a surprise. You knew it was a possibility from the very first time we were together. I've always been up front with you. This is my decision. The sooner you accept it, the easier it will be for you. Goodbye."

When she was certain the call was done, Gabrielle poked her head into Claire's room.

"Everything okay?" she asked. "That sounded a little rough."

"It comes with the territory," Claire replied, sounding tired. "You know that as well as I do, Gabby. Some people tend to get a little...attached."

"That sounded like it was teetering on the line between attachment and stalkerish. Do you want to talk about it?"

"Not really," Claire admitted. "I've got a guy picking me up at seven. That only gives me two hours to get ready. I'd rather focus on that."

"You and me both," Gabrielle said. "I shouldn't set up two dates for one day. I'm wiped out from the beach. And now I've got to go clubbing until two a.m. My calves are going to be screaming tomorrow."

"Tough lives we lead," Claire said with a lopsided grin.

Gabby smiled back. She liked her friend most when she was like this: playful and self-deprecating. It made it hard to get jealous even if Claire was gorgeous—a petite, blonde-haired, busty, sun-kissed Southern California goddess. Just a shade over five feet tall and hovering around 100 pounds, she was dynamite in a tiny package. But it was when she let down her guard that her charm really shined through. Only a few guys ever got to see that side of her.

"Listen," Gabrielle said. "How about we take a break tomorrow—just you, me, some mimosas, and something binge-worthy?"

"That sounds awesome," Claire said. "I could really use some downtime. Everything feels so heightened these days. I wish people would chill, you know?"

"I do. So tomorrow is officially Gabby and Claire's Day of Chill. Deal?"

"Deal," Claire agreed. "At least until six. I have a dinner."

Gabby gave her an incredulous look but she couldn't keep a straight face and they both burst out laughing.

CHAPTER ONE

For about the fourth time in the last hour, the same thought passed through Jessie Hunt's head.

I hate this place.

"This place" was an official WITSEC safe house. Though she despised being in the sterile tract home with US Marshals always around, she couldn't really argue that it wasn't necessary. After all, it had been less than two weeks since she escaped an attack by her murderous serial killer father, Xander Thurman, who had been hunting for her for months.

And just days after that, his most ardent admirer, another killer named Bolton Crutchfield, had escaped from a psychiatric prison facility, along with four other dangerous prisoners. Two had been captured. But in addition to Crutchfield, two others were still on the loose.

So Jessie wasn't in a position to quarrel when Captain Roy Decker, her boss at LAPD, ordered her to do whatever the marshals with the Witness Security Program instructed until the situation was resolved. And that meant essentially living under house arrest while she was on a mandated leave of absence from her work as a forensic profiler.

She wasn't even technically a witness in a pending trial. But because of the imminent threat to her life, her work in law enforcement, and her connection to both the LAPD and the FBI, an exception had been made.

Until her father and Crutchfield were captured or killed, she was stuck. She spent her days following case updates online, broken up by frequent, near-frenzied workout sessions and self-defense training that did little to mitigate her stir-craziness.

The ten-week training program she'd recently taken at the FBI Academy in Quantico, Virginia, had provided her with effective fighting skills and new profiling techniques. But it hadn't taught her how to deal with the crushing boredom of being housebound for twenty-four hours a day.

The house itself was perfectly nice, located on a quiet residential block in the West Los Angeles neighborhood of Palms. In the late-spring mornings, she sipped her coffee and watched parents walk their children to the elementary school a few blocks away.

The house was at the end of a cul-de-sac, where it could be more easily secured and protected. But that meant there wasn't much to see most days. Usually around mid-morning, she'd go outside for a swim in the pool, which was covered by a large tarp, theoretically for shade but actually to undermine the prying eyes of neighbors.

Things were even worse now that Kat had left. For a few days her friend had been allowed to stay at the house as well, in part because authorities feared Bolton Crutchfield might come after her too. After all, Kat Gentry had been head of security at NRD—short for Non-Rehabilitative Division—the facility at the Department State Hospital-Metropolitan in Norwalk that Crutchfield and the other prisoners had escaped from. There was concern that some of them might want payback.

But when Kat mentioned she might take a long trip to Europe to clear her head, the marshals leapt at the idea as both a way to keep her off the radar and to reduce their security costs. Jessie still recalled their conversation from several days ago.

"Don't you think this is kind of running away from your problems?" Jessie had asked, realizing the question would likely put her friend on the defensive.

Kat looked at her quizzically. Even before she replied, Jessie knew she'd made a mistake. After all, Katherine Gentry was a former Marine who still bore the shrapnel scars from an IED explosion on her face. She had maintained a lockdown facility housing some of society's worst until her most trusted lieutenant, Ernie Cortez, had betrayed her, enabling the escape. She was tough as nails and Jessie knew it.

"I think I'm entitled to a little personal time," Kat said, refusing to defend herself beyond that. "If I thought the marshals would let you, I'd suggest you come with me."

"Believe me, I'd love that," Jessie replied, relieved her friend hadn't been more defensive. "But the truth is, until my father and Crutchfield are caught, I'm not going to sleep easy, no matter what continent I'm on. Once we come up with a plan to catch these guys, I'm all over it. I need to finish this so I can have some kind of life."

"It doesn't seem like there's much of a plan in place," Kat noted wryly.

"Nope," Jessie agreed. "And don't think that hasn't been on my mind. The only saving grace is that I know my father is too injured to come after me just yet. When I last saw him, he was jumping out a fourth-floor window, and that was before he was injured already in the stomach, shoulder, and head. He's going to be out of commission for a little while."

"But Bolton Crutchfield won't be," Kat reminded her. "He's perfectly healthy and raring to go. And he has...assets at his disposal."

Kat didn't elaborate beyond that but she didn't need to. They both knew what she meant. In addition to the two escapees he might have at his disposal, there was also Ernie, Kat's former second-in-command at NRD.

While Kat was attending the funeral ceremony for Jessie's adoptive parents, Ernie, an imposing physical specimen at six foot six and 250 pounds, murdered multiple NRD security officers, then released Crutchfield and the others. It was days afterward that the FBI was able to uncover what never showed up in the background check Kat had conducted when hiring him.

When Ernie was eleven years old, he'd spent a year in a juvenile psychiatric facility after stabbing another kid multiple times in the abdomen with a screwdriver. Luckily for him, the other boy survived.

Ernie served his time without incident. After his release and a family move, he had no further problems. His juvenile records were sealed when he turned eighteen. With no other red flags on his record, all that remained was a sterling resume in the US Army, followed by stints as a private security contractor and a prison guard at a supermax prison in Colorado.

If Kat had access to his psychiatric records from the juvenile detention center, she would have learned that the medical personnel viewed him as a sociopath with an amazing facility to control and hide his violent predilections.

The final line of his release papers read, "It is the opinion of this physician that subject Cortez poses a continuing risk to the community. He has learned to conceal his desires but it is likely that at some point, soon or perhaps well in the future, the same psychiatric issues that led to his placement at this facility will reassert themselves. Unfortunately, our current system makes no accommodation for that possibility and requires that he be released forthwith. Follow-up treatment, while not mandated, is highly recommended."

No further treatment occurred. When Ernie became a guard at NRD and began interacting with Bolton Crutchfield, a master manipulator, he fell under his sway. But he never let on, continuing to do his job and interact positively with the co-workers he would eventually kill.

Kat blamed herself for all their deaths, though there was no way she could have anticipated them. Jessie had tried multiple times to assuage her guilt, to no avail.

"I'm a forensic profiler who is trained to pick up things like sociopathic tendencies," she'd said. "I interacted with him on over a dozen occasions and I never once suspected him. I don't see how you could have."

"It doesn't matter," Kat insisted. "I was responsible for those officers' safety and for keeping those inmates secure. I failed on both fronts. I deserve the blame."

That conversation was three days ago. Now Kat was somewhere in France, unaware that the Marshal Service had requested that Interpol assign an undercover officer to tail her for her own protection. For her part, Jessie was stuck lying on plastic pool furniture within shouting distance of freeway traffic. She had no one to talk to, hardly any privacy, and little to keep her mind from going to dark places. In the more self-pitying moments, she felt like she was being victimized all over again.

As she headed inside to grab herself a snack, she pulled on the cover-up one of the marshals had bought her the other day. He wasn't given detailed instructions so how it fit wasn't his fault. But Jessie couldn't help but be frustrated that the thing barely went down to her hips and was somehow still bulky. A lean five foot ten, she needed something twice as long and half as wide. She put her shoulder-length brown hair in a ponytail and tried to keep her green eyes from looking too annoyed as she stepped inside.

Entering the house, she saw the marshal who was standing near the sliding door turn his head slightly. He was clearly listening to some message in his earpiece. His body tensed up involuntarily at whatever he'd been told. Jessie knew something was up even before she entered the kitchen.

He didn't say anything to her so she continued toward the kitchen, pretending to be oblivious to whatever was going on. Uncertain if the message was about a breach of the house, she looked around for something to protect herself with in case Crutchfield had found her. Resting on a console table in the dining room near the kitchen entrance was a glass snow globe of San Francisco, about the size of a cantaloupe.

As she fleetingly wondered why San Francisco would have snow, she grabbed the globe and placed it behind her back. Then she stepped into the kitchen with her weight on the balls of her feet, her body torqued for action and her eyes darting back and forth in search of any threat. At the far end of the kitchen, a door opened.

CHAPTER TWO

As Jessie waited to see who it was, she realized she'd stopped breathing and forced herself to exhale slowly and quietly.

Stepping briskly into the room, without a hint of apprehension, was Frank Corcoran. The supervising marshal on her detail, Corcoran was all business. Square-jawed and square-framed, he wore a navy suit with a white shirt and perfectly knotted black tie. His neatly trimmed mustache had the first hints of gray at the edges, as did his short-cropped black hair.

"Have a seat, Ms. Hunt," he said without a trace of casualness. "We need to talk. And you can put down the snow globe. I promise you won't need it."

Placing the globe on the kitchen table while pointedly refusing to ask how he'd known about it, Jessie sat down, wondering what fresh hell he was about to reveal. Xander Thurman had already murdered her adoptive parents. He'd nearly killed two cops trying to get to her in her own apartment. Bolton Crutchfield's violent escape from NRD had led to the deaths of six guards. Had one of the remaining escapees found Kat in Europe? Had they gone after her friend and sometime partner, LAPD Detective Ryan Hernandez, whom she hadn't heard from in days? She prepared herself for the worst.

"I have some updates for you," Corcoran said, when he realized Jessie wasn't going to ask any questions.

"Okay."

I spoke with your captain," he said, pulling out a scrap of paper and reading from it. "He wanted to convey the well wishes of the entire precinct. He said they are following every available lead and he hopes you won't have to sit tight for too much longer."

Jessie could tell from Corcoran's skeptical tone of voice and his slightly raised eyebrows that he didn't share Captain Decker's view of the situation.

"You're less optimistic than he, I gather?"

"That's the next update," he replied, not technically answering her question. "We've had no luck finding Mr. Crutchfield. While two escapees have been captured, as you know, two others are still at large, not to mention Mr. Cortez."

"Did the captured men provide any useful information since you last updated me?"

"Unfortunately no," he conceded. "Both men still say the same thing—that they all went their separate ways within minutes of their escape. Neither of these men even knew it was happening until they were released from their cells."

"So it was likely only Crutchfield and Cortez who planned this?"

"That's what we think," Corcoran said. "Nonetheless, we have a massive, ongoing manhunt for all the escapees. In addition to LAPD, the Sheriff's Department, CHP, the CBI, and FBI are all involved, as is, of course, the Marshals Service."

"I noticed you mentioned that you're searching for the escapees," she said. "What about Xander Thurman?"

"What about him?"

"Well, he's a serial killer too. He tried to kill me and two LAPD officers and he's on the loose. How many people do you have looking for him?"

Corcoran looked at her as if he was surprised that he even needed to make his next comment.

"Based on your description of his injuries, we view him as a less immediate threat. And your status in WITSEC makes us less concerned about him generally. Besides, right now our priority is on the multiple escapees from a criminal psychiatric facility, not on a man no one even knows is out there."

"You mean your search is being media and politics driven," Jessie noted pointedly.

"That is one, not inaccurate, way to characterize it."

Jessie appreciated his honesty. And for someone in his position, she couldn't really argue that it was an unreasonable use of resources. She decided to let it go for now.

"Any potential leads?" Jessie asked doubtfully.

"We believe our best efforts center around Mr. Cortez. The thinking is that he would have made plans for after the escape. We're checking his bank records, credit card purchases, and phone GPS data in the weeks prior to the breakout. So far, we haven't found anything as helpful as plane tickets."

"You won't," Jessie muttered.

"Why do you say that?"

"Cortez will stick close to Crutchfield. And I guarantee you—Bolton Crutchfield isn't going anywhere."

"How can you be so sure?" Corcoran demanded.

"Because he's not done with me yet."

*

That night Jessie couldn't sleep. After tossing and turning for what felt like hours, she got out of bed and headed to the kitchen to refill her empty water glass.

As she walked down the carpeted hallway from the bedroom she immediately sensed something was wrong. The marshal usually stationed in a chair where the hallway met the living room was nowhere to be found. Jessie considered returning to her room to get a gun before remembering that she didn't actually have one. The Marshals Service had "secured" it until further notice.

Instead she pressed her back against the wall of the hallway, ignoring her quickly beating heart as she tiptoed toward the empty chair. As she got closer, with the aid of the moonlight streaming in through the windows, she saw a dark, damp stain on the cream-colored carpeting. The wide range of the spray suggested it wasn't accidentally dropped wine. She also noticed a consistent trail of it extending out of sight.

Jessie poked her head around the corner to see the marshal lying on his back against the far wall, where he'd apparently been dragged. His throat was slit all the way across. Next to him on the ground was his service weapon.

Jessie felt a surge of anxiety-laden adrenaline, which made her fingers tingle. Reminding herself to stay focused, she knelt down and surveyed the room as she waited for her body to settle down. It took less time than she expected.

With no one in sight, she darted out and grabbed the gun. Glancing down, she saw a path of bloody footprints headed away from the marshal's body in the direction of the adjoining dining room. Staying crouched behind the sofa, she scurried along until she could see into the room clearly.

Another marshal lay on the ground there. This one was face down with a quickly expanding pool of blood pouring from his neck and forming a puddle around his face and torso.

Jessie forced herself not to linger on the image as she followed the bloody footprints from that room into the sunroom, which led to the backyard pool. The sliding door was open and a slight breeze blew the hanging curtains inward, making them billow like low-hanging clouds.

She checked the room. It was empty so she moved over to the sliding door to peek outside. A suited body was visible, bobbing face down in the water, which was quickly turning a pinkish-red. That's when she heard someone clear his throat behind her.

She whirled around, cocking the gun at the same time. Facing her at the far end of the room were both Bolton Crutchfield and her father, Xander Thurman, who looked shockingly good considering that only weeks ago, he'd been shot in the gut and the shoulder, likely fractured his skull, and jumped out a fourth-floor window. Both men were holding long hunting knives.

Her father smiled as he silently mouthed the word "Junebug," his pet name for her as a child. Jessie lifted the gun and prepared to fire. As her finger began to squeeze the trigger, Crutchfield spoke.

"I promised that I'd be seeing you, Miss Jessie," he said, his demeanor as placid as it had been when he spoke to her through the thick glass barrier of his cell.

His weeks of freedom hadn't made him any less soft. At five foot eight and about 150 pounds, he was less physically formidable than Jessie. His pudgy face made him look a decade younger than his thirty-five years and his brown hair, parted neatly to the side, reminded her of the boys in the math club back at middle school. Only his steely brown eyes hinted at what he was truly capable of.

"It looks like you've fallen in with a bad crowd," she said in a frustratingly shaky voice as she nodded at her father.

"That's what I love about you, Miss Jessie," Crutchfield said admiringly. "You never back down, even when you're in a hopeless situation."

"You may want to rethink that," Jessie pointed out. "You've both brought knives to a gunfight."

"So impish," Crutchfield marveled, looking over at Thurman with appreciation.

Her father nodded, still silent. Then both men returned their attention to her. Simultaneously, their smiles disappeared.

"It's time, Miss Jessie," Crutchfield said as both men moved toward her in tandem.

She fired at her father first, three in the chest, before turning her attention to Crutchfield. Without hesitation, she pumped three bullets into his torso. The air was full of acrid smoke and the echo of her shots.

But neither man stopped or even slowed down. How was that possible? Even with bulletproof vests, they should have been staggering.

She was out of bullets but pulled the trigger anyway, unsure what else to do. As the two men advanced on her with their knives lifted high above their heads, she tossed away the gun and assumed a defensive stance, fully aware that it was a futile gesture. The knives came slicing down, hard and fast.

*

With a gasp Jessie sat bolt upright in bed. She was drenched in sweat and breathing heavily. Looking around the room, she saw she was alone. The shutters on the windows were still nailed shut to prevent access. Her bedroom door still had the chair propped under the knob as an extra security precaution. The clock read 1:39 a.m.

There was a soft knock on the door.

"You okay in there, Ms. Hunt?" one of the marshals asked. "I heard a noise."

"Just a bad dream," she called out, seeing no reason to lie about what he likely already suspected.

"Okay. Let me know if you need anything."

"Thanks," she said, listening for the familiar creak of the floorboard beneath the carpet as he walked away.

She slid her legs out of bed and sat quietly for a moment, allowing her heart rate and breathing to return to something close to normal. She stood up and headed to the bathroom. A shower was in order, as was a change of the damp sheets.

As she crossed the room, she couldn't help but wander over to the one window where the shutter was tilted open slightly to allow in a bit of light. She swore she saw the silhouette of someone in the shadows of the trees beyond the pool. Even after assuring herself that it was either a tree trunk or a marshal, she felt unsettled.

Somewhere out there two serial killers were on the loose. And both of them were looking for her. There was no getting around the fact that even in a completely secured safe house with all this protection around, she was a sitting duck.

*

Gabrielle and her date for the night, Carter, arrived back at the house just after 2 a.m. They were both a little drunk and she had to remind him again to keep his voice down so as not to wake up Claire.

They stumbled clumsily through the hall until they got to her bedroom, where they shared a long kiss. Gabby pulled back and gave him her best "come hither" smile. He returned the smile, although not too eagerly. She liked that. He was older—in his late forties—and able to control his enthusiasm better than some of the newly minted tech boys she went out with.

He was good-looking in a distinguished kind of way and reminded her of some of her dad's friends, the ones who snuck glances at her when they thought she wasn't looking. He waited for her to resume the kissing. When she held off teasingly to find out how he'd react, he finally spoke.

"Nice place you've got here," he said in a mock whisper.

If all goes well, you'll be helping pay for it for a while.

She managed to keep that thought to herself and responded with a less opportunistic, "Thanks. There's one part I'm especially anxious to show you."

She nodded to the bed.

"Are you suggesting I check it out? I really feel like a guided tour might be in order."

"Why don't you get comfortable over there? I'll make a brief sojourn to the restroom to freshen up and join you momentarily."

Carter smiled in agreement and walked over to the side of the bed. As he slid off his shoes and began untucking his shirt, Gabby headed to the bathroom the housemates shared. She turned on the light and cast one last seductive look at him before closing the door behind her.

Once inside, she went straight to the mirror. Before retouching any makeup, she wanted to check her teeth. A cursory glance showed nothing visible between them. She took a quick swig of mouthwash and was swishing it around, preparing to add a hint of extra smokiness to her eyelids, when she noticed an arm draped over the freestanding tub behind her.

She turned around, surprised. It wasn't like Claire to take a bath at this hour. Usually she crashed as soon as she got home, sometimes not even changing out of her clothes. If she was lying in the tub with the lights out, it likely meant she was totally smashed.

Gabby tiptoed over, praying that she'd only have to deal with a passed-out housemate and not a vomit-covered tub. As she peeked over the edge of the tub, what she saw was far worse.

Claire was still dressed in the miniskirt she'd worn to go out that night. She was lying face up in the tub, with her glassy eyes wide open, covered in blood. Her face was streaked with it and it had formed a thick, goopy sauce in her hair. The blood was everywhere but it seemed to be mostly coming from her throat, which was mangled by what looked to be multiple deep stab wounds.

Gabby stared at her and only realized that she had been screaming when Carter appeared next to her, shaking her shoulders and asking what was wrong. One look at the tub gave him an answer. He stumbled backward in shock before pulling his cell phone out of his pocket.

"Come out of there," he told her, grabbing her wrist and tearing her away from the horror in front of her. "Go sit on the bed. I'm calling nine-one-one."

She stopped screaming, grateful to have an instruction to follow. She shuffled numbly over to the bed, where she sat down, staring at the floor but not really seeing anything. In the background, she heard his voice, distant and tinny.

"I need to report a murder. There's a woman dead in the bathtub here. It looks like she was stabbed."

Gabby closed her eyes tight but it didn't help. The image of Claire, helpless and limp in the bathroom only feet away, was burned into her mind.

CHAPTER THREE

The marshal was being an asshole. All Jessie wanted was to go for a jog. He kept using the phrase "not advisable," which really mean "not allowed." He pointed to the treadmill in the corner of the living room as if that should answer all her concerns.

"But I need some fresh air," she said, aware that she sounded borderline whiny.

The marshal, known only to her as Murph, was not the chattiest guy ever, a frustrating trait since he was the primary duty agent in her security detail. Short and trim with light brown hair that looked like it was cut weekly, he seemed content to avoid speaking at all if possible. As if to prove it, he nodded at the backyard in response. Jessie tried to recall if he was one of the marshals murdered in last night's nightmare, part of her wishing it had been.

The truth was Jessie didn't really just need fresh air or a jog. She wanted to visit the local hospitals again to see if anyone matching her father's description had shown up since the last time she checked, before she was placed in the safe house. Her sometime partner, Detective Ryan Hernandez, was supposed to be keeping her looped in on that. But since she hadn't been able to reach out to anyone lately, including him, she had no idea if he'd met with any success.

Jessie was pretty sure the marshal knew her true intentions but that didn't make her any less annoyed. She was going stir-crazy cooped up in this house. And though she knew she was being kept here for her own protection, she'd reached the limits of her patience, especially after last night's dream. She decided something had to change. And there was only one way to make that happen.

"I want to see Captain Decker," she said firmly.

The marshal seemed reluctant to respond, hoping he could ignore this demand as he had all the others. But of course, he couldn't. Jessie couldn't force them to let her go on a walk or make a trip to the grocery store. But if she made a formal request to see her supervisor and it could be accommodated safely, the service was required to do so.

Slowly, and with a scowl, the marshal raised his hand and spoke into the communication device connected to his wrist.

"Jabberjay requests an authorized sit-down. Please advise."

As Jessie waited for the response, she stayed quiet, choosing not to comment on the less-than-endearing code name she'd apparently been assigned.

*

Ninety minutes later she sat in a small conference room in a quiet corner of Central Community Police Station in downtown Los Angeles, waiting for Captain Decker to join her. The marshal named Murph, who had accompanied her here from the house, stood in the back of the room, clearly still annoyed at having to be there.

The process to get to the place, known generally as Central Station, had been cumbersome. After getting formal authorization for the trip from Corcoran, a team had to be assembled and a route chosen. Much of that had been pre-planned but final choices had to be selected.

Jessie was instructed to wear a wig, along with a cap pulled down low over her eyes. Then the vehicle, driven by a marshal named Toomey, with Murph in the passenger seat, set out. A second car followed at a distance with two more agents inside. Two additional agents remained at the house to keep it secure.

Even though it was mid-morning and traffic was comparatively light, with all the last-second turns and doubling back, the drive took over forty-five minutes. Once at the station, the car pulled into the garage and they had to stay in it until it was formally cleared by two uniformed officers who didn't know why they were doing it other than "orders from on high."

Only then was Jessie whisked through a side entrance, still wearing the wig, a cap, and a bulky jacket with the collar zipped up all the way to disguise her general size and her neck, which might have revealed her gender. She was held back at various points, until hallways were clear enough for her to pass.

When she finally made it to the conference room, Murph joined her inside while Toomey stood guard at the door. Since Toomey was six foot four and easily 220 pounds, with a completely shaved head and a permanent scowl, Jessie doubted anyone would try to enter without permission. One of the remaining marshals waited outside at the entrance from the garage to the building and the fourth circled the block slowly in his car, keeping an eye out for anything unusual.

Jessie forced down the guilt she felt at being the cause of all this action. She knew she'd probably just spent thousands of dollars of taxpayer money for what seemed like a petulant demand. But there was more to it than that. If she could get Captain Decker on board with her plan, the cost of this short drive might be repaid hundreds of times over. But she had to convince him first.

"You know," Murph said quietly from the corner, speaking for the first time since they'd entered the room. "We're actually trying to help keep you safe. You aren't required to fight us every step of the way."

"I'm not trying to fight you," she insisted. "I'm trying to help. And despite what your boss might think, I'm actually in a pretty good position to do it."

"What do you mean?" he asked as the door to the room opened and Captain Decker walked in.

"You're about to find out," Jessie promised.

Captain Roy Decker, appearing winded and irked, glared at her. Not yet sixty but looking well past it, the captain of Central Station was tall and thin, with only a few small patches of hair preventing total baldness. His face was lined with creases developed through years of stressful work. His sharp nose and beady eyes reminded her of a bird on the lookout for prey.

"You okay, Captain?" Jessie asked. "You look like you ran here."

"When you hear that your forensic profiler, who is supposed to be hidden away in witness protection, is down the hall, you get a little giddy-up in your step. Care to tell me what's so important that I had to come to this godforsaken corner of the station, where there's more asbestos than oxygen in the air?"

Out of the corner of her eye, Jessie saw Murph shift uncomfortably from one foot to the other and smiled to herself. He didn't yet know of Decker's gift for overstatement.

"Absolutely sir. But before I do, can I ask how things are going with the hunt for…everyone?"

Decker sighed heavily. For a second it looked like he might not respond. But finally he settled into the chair across from her and spoke.

"Not great, actually," he admitted. "You know we caught one NRD escapee, Jackson, the first day. We caught another one, Gimbel, a couple of days after that. But since then, despite dozens of credible leads, we've had no luck finding the other two guys, nor Crutchfield and Cortez."

"Do you think they're all together?" Jessie asked, already aware that the Marshals Service didn't.

"No. We've seen surveillance footage of Stokes and De La Rosa near the hospital when they first broke out and they were each on their own. We haven't found any footage of Crutchfield and Cortez but the working theory is that they're still together."

"Hmm," Jessie said. "If only you had some kind of human resource who was familiar with both men and could offer insight into their likely behavioral patterns."

The sarcasm, fully intended, dripped from her lips. Decker barely blinked.

"And if only that resource wasn't the target of the very men she was familiar with, we might take advantage of that knowledge," he replied.

They stared at each other silently for a moment, neither inclined to concede their point. Jessie finally relented, deciding that alienating the man whose authorization she needed wasn't advisable.

"What about Xander Thurman? Any more luck with him?"

"None. He's kept off the radar completely."

"Even with all his injuries?"

"We've been monitoring every hospital, urgent care center, and free clinic. We even sent alerts to veterinarians. There's been nothing."

"Then that means one of two things," Jessie concluded. "Either he has access to someone else with medical training, or someone at one of these places is lying, maybe under threat. There is no way he could have recovered from those injuries without help. It's not possible."

"I'm aware of that, Ms. Hunt. But this is the information we have right now."

"What if you had more?" she asked.

"What do you mean?" Decker asked.

19

"I know how he operates, just like I know how Crutchfield does. Crimes that might look unremarkable to most detectives could have markers I could identify with one of them. If I could check out recent case files and investigate the more promising leads, maybe we could catch a break."

From the back of the room, Murph spoke up.

"That seems unwise."

Jessie was happy to hear that. Nothing rankled Decker more than department outsiders offering their unsolicited two cents. Having him view the marshal as an interloper could only help her case. As she watched her boss frown, she stayed quiet, letting the dynamic percolate.

"What exactly did you have in mind?" Decker asked her through gritted teeth.

Jessie didn't wait for him to change his mind.

"I could look at violent attacks and murders in the last few weeks to see if any of them have the hallmarks of either killer. If any of them are a match, I can pursue the most promising leads."

Decker sat silently, apparently contemplating the idea. Murph, however, did not stay quiet.

"You can't seriously be entertaining this after all the effort the Marshals Service went to in order to secure a safe house for her."

Please keep arguing. You're only digging your own grave.

Decker seemed to be fighting an internal war with himself. It was clear that, despite his annoyance with Murph, he felt the man made a good point. But she could also tell that something else was at play in his head, something Jessie apparently wasn't aware of.

"Here's the thing," he eventually said. "As I mentioned, we have lots of leads—maybe too many of them. Just trying to cull through them has been challenging. We've enlisted the sheriff's department and other neighboring police departments. Even the local FBI has pitched in, offering a few agents on cases they deem relevant. We're just spread so damn thin right now. It's not like all the other criminals have taken a vacation just because we've got five additional psychos on the loose. There was a gang hit two days ago. Someone is leaving hypodermic needles on local playgrounds. Your old pal Detective Hernandez is tied up with a triple homicide that has him in Topanga Canyon today. And, oh by the way, we're in the second week of a massive measles outbreak."

"What are you saying, Captain?" Murph asked. For the first time, Jessie thought she sensed a hint of resignation in his voice.

Decker finally spilled the secret he'd been keeping up to this point.

"There is actually a case that came in overnight that I think you could be helpful on, Hunt. It happened in Studio City so North Hollywood Station is handling it. But the FBI has taken an interest and assigned an agent to look into it. I was thinking of pairing you with him."

"What's the case?" Jessie asked, keeping her voice even despite the excitement rising in her belly.

"A stabbing—pretty gruesome. No motive or suspects yet. But both your boys are big knife fans, right?"

"That's true," she agreed.

"It could be totally unrelated," he conceded. "But it's the first attack I've come across that seems to fit the profile."

"So you plan to let her go into the field?" Murph asked, though he knew the answer.

"Well, I figure that with an FBI agent as a partner and multiple US marshals keeping tabs on her, she should be safe. Is that an unfair assumption?"

"Captain Decker," Murph replied neutrally, "it is the general view of the Service that no protectee is ever truly safe. And it is my personal opinion that putting this protectee in the field, investigating a murder potentially committed by one of the very people we're trying to protect her from, is singularly unsafe."

"But," Jessie interjected, finally ready to make the point she'd been holding in reserve, "it's not really any worse than the status quo. For almost two weeks now, I've been under protection. But no one has uncovered anything about the men pursuing me that might change the status quo. It's costing the city, the LAPD, and the Marshals Service a small fortune, with no end in sight. The way things are going, I might truly have to get a new identity…for the second time in my life!"

"That not how we view it…" Murph started to say.

"Please let me finish, Marshal," she said, all trace of snark or cockiness gone from her voice now. "This has to end. I'm having nightmares every night about my protective detail being slaughtered. I jump at every unexpected sound and cringe at every sudden movement. I am a prisoner in that house even though I haven't done anything wrong. It's not how I want to live. I'd rather try to catch these guys and end up dead than spend the rest of my days living in fear. I have the skills and the inside knowledge to find both the men who mean me harm. Allow me to use them. It's not an unreasonable request."

Decker and Murph exchanged looks. After what felt like an eternity, the marshal spoke.

"I'll square it with Corcoran," he relented before adding, "if you agree to certain terms."

"What terms?" Jessie asked, though she was willing to agree to almost anything at this point."

"Your protective detail remains with you at all times—no attempts to lose us. You continue to spend nights at the safe house. You agree to all security precautions in the field, even evasive maneuvers you might consider excessive. You defer to the marshals' judgment in any field scenario, no matter how overcautious you deem it to be. If we say leave, you agree to leave, no questions asked. Can you agree to these terms, Ms. Hunt?"

"I can," she said without hesitation, whether she planned to adhere to them or not.

"Then, pending authorization from my superior, you can proceed."

Jessie looked at Decker, who appeared to be fighting off a grin.

"Care to meet your temporary partner?" he asked.

CHAPTER FOUR

Jessie wasn't impressed.

The FBI agent on loan to the department for the stabbing case looked like an old baseball player called into the game because all the starters were injured. As she walked over to meet him, Jessie noted that the guy, who appeared to be in his late thirties or early forties, had a surprising paunch for an FBI agent.

In addition, his hair, unexpectedly longish and disheveled, was almost completely silver. His weathered face and salty scent suggested he spent more time surfing that doing case work. His blazer was frayed at the collar and his tie was only loosely knotted. And even though it was still morning, he'd already accumulated an impressive array of food stains on his rumpled slacks.

"Jack Dolan," he said, extending his hand as she approached but not offering any greeting beyond that.

"Jessie Hunt," she said, trying not to wince at his tight grip.

"Ah, yes. The infamous forensic profiler slash serial killer's daughter slash psycho whisperer in hiding from men who go bump in the night."

"That's what it says on my business card," Jessie replied acidly, not enamored by all the assumptions this guy was making right off the bat.

"Agent Dolan," Decker interjected, cutting off the icy exchange, "as the Studio City stabbing has several potential characteristics of both Xander Thurman and Bolton Crutchfield, we've decided that Ms. Hunt should join you to assess how likely it is that one of them is responsible."

Dolan looked at Decker, then at Jessie, and finally, at Murph.

"So," he asked, apparently confused. "Am I babysitting her now? Or are we tag-teaming it?"

Jessie opened her mouth, uncertain what she would say other than that it would include expletives. But before she could get a word out, Decker jumped in.

"Consider her your partner for the duration of the case. I assume you'd have your partner's back, Agent Dolan? This is no different."

Dolan held his tongue. Out of the corner of her eye, Jessie saw Murph fight off a grin. She turned to Decker.

"Can I speak to you privately for a moment?" she asked.

He nodded and they started to step out into the hall.

"Hold on," Murph said. "The agent and I will step outside. You two talk in here; the fewer people who see you, the better."

After they left, Jessie turned, blazing-eyed, to Decker.

"Is this some kind of punishment? Is that why you're putting me with this guy? Can't you just pull Hernandez off the case he's working and have me team up with him?"

"Detective Hernandez is unavailable," he relied tersely. "We don't just 'pull' detectives off triple homicides to accommodate the whims of other staffers. You shouldn't expect to hear from him any time soon. If you do, it means he's not doing his job. Besides, Dolan is more than qualified for this case. And he's who the Bureau made available. So find a way to work with him. Otherwise you can go back to the safe house. It's your call, Hunt."

*

The drive to Studio City was especially uncomfortable.

Dolan clearly wasn't happy that he had to be transported in the back seat of a sedan driven a US marshal. Murph and Toomey weren't enthused about chauffeuring around two surly investigators. And Jessie was annoyed by pretty much everything.

Despite what Decker had said, she felt like she had three babysitters in the car, with two more in a vehicle behind them. Her "partner" apparently considered her involvement in the case tokenism. And the marshals obviously resented being highly trained valets. By the time they got to the crime scene, everyone was on edge.

Toomey found the house easily. It was the charming, Spanish-style one-story home with a half dozen police cars and reams of yellow police tape in front of it. There were also two television trucks. He drove past all of them and parked halfway down the block, where they wouldn't be seen.

"How are we handling this?" he asked the rest of them. "We can't have Hunt be seen walking into that house. If this is the handiwork of either Thurman or Crutchfield, they'll be watching closely to see if she shows up. And even if it's not theirs, we don't want her face splashed all over the news."

Jessie waited to see if any of them would suggest the obvious solution. When no one did, she spoke up.

"Pull around back," she instructed. "There was no driveway. That means there's garage access from the alley. It'll be closed off to TV crews and they can't get those wide vans back there anyway. We should be able to get in without any cameras getting close."

No one seemed to have any objections so Toomey started the car up again and did as she recommended. He radioed the other marshals to let them know the plan and advised them to remain on the main street.

Sure enough, the narrow alley was blocked off by patrol cars at either end. They pulled over and got out. Murph and Dolan flashed their badges to the nearest officer, who let them pass without asking for ID from either Toomey or Jessie, who was reluctant to reveal her identity to anyone, even a cop.

They walked through the back gate and up the porch steps to the entrance, where another officer asked for identification. He was less reluctant to let them pass without seeing everyone's. But Dolan leaned in and whispered something Jessie couldn't hear to the officer, who nodded and stepped back to let them through.

As they stepped through the door, Jessie tried to block out all the hassles of the morning and focus on her surroundings. She was on a case now and the victim, whoever it was, deserved her full attention.

The back door opened into the kitchen, which was contemporary and well-appointed with all the latest appliances. In fact, everything looked so pristine that she suspected it had all been redone in the last six months. Something about the place reminded her of the brand new McMansions of all those newly wealthy couples in Orange County, where she'd lived briefly before learning her now ex-husband, Kyle Voss, was a violent sociopath.

"Who lives here?' she asked no one in particular.

A youngish-looking uniformed officer with sandy blond hair standing in the corner heard and walked over.

"I thought the detectives were all done," he said.

"FBI is helping out," Dolan volunteered, flashing his badge and looking at the young cop's name tag. "What can you tell us, Officer Martin?"

"Yes sir," Martin replied. "The home is rented by two women. Gabrielle Cantu and Claire Stanton. Stanton is the victim. She was twenty-three years old. She was found early this morning by Cantu and her date."

"Where is Cantu now?" Jessie asked.

"At her date's place," Officer Martin answered. "He lives just over the hill off Mulholland Drive. She doesn't have any family in town so he said he'd let her stay there until she felt better. She obviously isn't comfortable coming back here any time soon."

"Where was Stanton's body found?" Dolan asked.

"In the bathroom," Martin said. "I'll show you."

As he led them down the hall, Jessie noticed that marshals Murph and Toomey kept their distance. They seemed less interested in the minutiae of the case than in scoping out everyone else—officers, crime scene folks—in the house. Even in a home filled with law enforcement, they were all considered potential threats to the protectee, in this case, her.

She wondered what kind of business Gabrielle and Claire were in that they could afford to rent a place like this in their early twenties. She supposed they could both be associates at white shoe law firms.

But her experience in this job so far told her they were more likely models or trust fund babies. They might be actresses too. And though it was a stereotype, the fact that they lived in the San Fernando Valley increased the chances that they were performers of an adult variety.

The living room had a big-screen television with surround sound speakers, leather couches, and a bar. As they entered the hall to the bedrooms, Jessie noted that there wasn't much to speak of in the way of art. There were toys and tech but nothing that suggested the residents had a long-term investment in the place.

When they reached the first bedroom, Officer Martin stopped.

"This was Claire Stanton's room," he said. "The bathroom connects with the other girl's bedroom. That's how she found her. Stanton was in the tub."

"Has the crime scene team finished up in there?" Jessie asked. "Is it okay if we go in?"

"Yes. The body has been transported. I can have the lead CSU investigator text you the photos if you like."

"Please," Jessie said, stepping into the bathroom.

The body may have been gone but the remnants of the carnage remained. While the rest of the bathroom looked unaffected, the tub, an old-fashioned freestanding type in the middle of the room, was covered in blood, much of which had pooled into a dark, viscous puddle near the drain.

As Jessie studied the scene, the photos from CSI popped up on her phone. She pulled them up while Dolan, who had gotten the same message, did the same on his.

In the first wide shot, Claire Stanton's body could be seen lying in the tub, face-up, with one arm extended over the edge. Her eyes were open and blood extended out from her neck, covering her chest and much of her face.

Despite that, Jessie could tell the girl had been beautiful, even more so than the busloads of pretty, aspiring Hollywood transplants. Blonde and petite, with toned, tanned limbs, she looked like the head cheerleader for a major university.

Additional photos showed close-ups of her neck and the damage done to it. While it was hard to be sure, on first inspection the wounds looked too jagged and rough to be caused by most knives. If Jessie had to guess, it looked more like the result of a screwdriver or…

"Keys," Dolan said.

"What?" Officer Martin said from the corner of the room.

"These injuries to her neck—they look like someone punctured it with long keys. Did the crime scene people have any guesses?"

"I wasn't around when they were evaluating the scene, Agent," he admitted.

"I think you're right," Jessie said. "The puncture marks look like they came at different angles and landed at different depths, almost as if the assailant was clutching multiple keys and jammed them all into her at the same time."

"I didn't know you were trained in crime scene analysis," Dolan said, his eyes raised skeptically.

"I'm not. But I am trained in seeing what's right in front of me," she retorted. "Also, I have some experience with knife attacks. More importantly, I am trained in psychological behavior. And based on the preliminary images here, I'd say we're likely dealing with a crime of passion rather than a preplanned assault."

"Why do you say that?" Dolan asked, not arguing.

"It's hard to imagine that someone planning ahead would choose keys as his method of attack. It's too messy and not a sure thing in terms of effectiveness. This feels more impromptu."

"A crime of passion?" Dolan repeated teasingly.

"It's a cliché, but yeah."

"That doesn't do much to support the theory that this was Crutchfield or Thurman," he noted. "From what I understand, they're both pretty meticulous."

"I'd agree that it makes it less likely."

"When did the call come in?" Dolan asked, turning his attention back to Officer Martin.

"A little after two in the morning. Cantu and her date had returned from a night out. She went into the bathroom and found her there. The guy, name of Carter Harrington, called nine-one-one."

Dolan walked around the bathroom for a few more seconds, looking bored.

"I think we've learned all we can here for the time being," he said, turning to Jessie. "What do you say we pay a visit to Gabrielle Cantu and see if she can provide a little color for us?"

Jessie nodded. She could sense him trying to move things along. If this case wasn't related to one of their outstanding serial killers, he clearly wanted to establish that quickly so he could dump the case and her along with it.

Though it struck her as cold, Jessie couldn't really blame him. He was after serial killers, not victims of clumsy key stabbings. And though she was loath to admit it, so was she.

CHAPTER FIVE

Whatever Gabrielle's date, Carter Harrington, did for a living, it paid well. The file she read on the way over only identified him as a "market investor," which could mean pretty much anything. His gated mansion on Briar Summit Drive, just off Mulholland Drive, was three stories tall with views of both the San Fernando Valley and the west side of Los Angeles. After they were buzzed in, the car with Jessie, Dolan, Murph, and Toomey eased down the long driveway to the parking circle in front of the home. The other marshals stayed outside the estate in their vehicle.

Carter Harrington came out to meet them. In his late forties, with salt and pepper hair and a fit physique that suggested he had lots of time to work out, Harrington was dressed casually in a polo shirt, tan slacks, and sandals. He smiled but it was clear from his red, bleary eyes that he'd been up all night.

"Carter Harrington," he said, extending his hand to Jessie first and then Dolan. "Sorry to meet you under these circumstances."

"Of course," Jessie said. "I'm Jessie Hunt with the LAPD and this is Jack Dolan of the FBI. Thanks for agreeing to see us so quickly."

"The FBI?" Harrington repeated, clearly surprised. "What about the detectives I talked to back at the house?"

"Oh, they're still the primary team on the investigation," Dolan said offhandedly. "But we're treating this as a multi-jurisdictional case. It's not that unusual."

Harrington seemed to accept that answer, though to Jessie's mind, it was a completely meaningless response, which was likely why Dolan said it.

"Where's Ms. Cantu?" she asked.

"Oh, right," he said, as if remembering why they were there in the first place. "Gabby's in the den, watching TV. She took a dose of Zoloft to settle her nerves but she's awake. You may have come at the ideal time. She's conscious but not agitated."

"Great," Dolan said. "Maybe you can give us your version of events on the way to see her."

"Sure," Harrington agreed, before noticing that only Murph was joining them as Toomey stood by the car.

"Um, what's up with your friend there?" he asked.

"Oh, he's here for moral support," Dolan said, straight-faced. "Don't pay him or this other fella any mind. Hunt and I are handling the particulars."

"Okay," Harrington said, leading them into the house without following up, though he was obviously perplexed by the whole thing.

"So," Jessie said, trying to move them past that bump in the road. "What were you doing at the house last night?"

"Right. That," he said, suddenly sounding uncomfortable as he walked along the wood-paneled hallway in front of them. "Gabby and I had been out that night. It was our first date and we went dancing at a few clubs. She invited me back to her place and I said sure. I was...settling into her bedroom while she went to the bathroom for a minute. Suddenly I heard her screaming and ran in. I found what your colleagues found. Her roommate was lying in the tub. I called nine-one-one right away. We went out to the living room and stayed there until help arrived."

"You'd never met Claire before?" Dolan asked.

Harrington came to a stop at the entrance to a large room Jessie assumed was the den. She could hear the sound of the TV in the background.

"No. I didn't even know Gabby had a housemate. Like I said, it was our first date. We'd only texted and talked on the phone before that."

"How did you meet Gabby?" Jessie asked, trying to sound as casual as possible.

"Through a dating site," he answered simply.

Does your wife know?

Jessie was tempted to ask the question out loud but decided to hold off for later if she needed it. The circle of pale skin on Harington's otherwise tanned ring finger suggested he was either very recently divorced or had taken his band off for this occasion.

"Care to make the introductions?" Dolan asked. "We don't want to freak her out by barging in."

30

"Sure," Harrington said, leading them into the cavernous den with its vaulted ceiling and floor to ceiling glass windows.

"Gabby," he said in a firm but gentle voice. "There are some folks here to see you."

A woman lying on the chaise lounge poked her head up. Though she looked wiped out and her eyes were red from what Jessie suspected was hours of crying, she was still stunning. More exotic and sultry than the all-American look of Claire, she had long dark hair that cascaded over her shoulders. As she sat up, Jessie saw that she had the kind of voluptuous body that might make someone like Carter Harrington hide his wedding ring.

"Who are they?" she asked, half-scared, half-defiant.

"My name is Jessie, Gabby," Jessie replied kindly, taking the initiative. "This is Jack. We're part of the team investigating what happened last night. We know you already answered some questions but we have a few more for you. Do you think you're up for that?"

"I guess," Gabby said reluctantly.

"Thanks," Jessie said, walking over and sitting on the couch closest to the chaise. "We'll try to keep it brief. I know you must be wiped out."

Gabby nodded, then looked to the corner of the room.

"Who's that?' she asked, indicating the US marshal who had positioned himself between the entrance to the den and the hallway they'd just passed through.

"That's Murph," Jessie said. "He's not a big talker. But he's really smart. He'll mostly just listen. Jack and I will be asking the questions. Why don't you have a seat, Jack?"

She gave Dolan her best "sit down—you're freaking her out" look. And, seeming to get it, he did so.

"So, let's start with this, Gabby," Jessie began. "Do you know if anyone had threatened Claire recently? Maybe an ex or a co-worker she'd had a falling out with?"

Gabby sat quietly for a moment, searching her memory.

"Not that I can think of," she finally said. "She was a sweetie. It was hard for anyone to truly get mad at her."

"Really?" Jessie pressed. "A pretty girl like her—I'd imagine she probably had to deal with letting down some disappointed pursuers."

31

"Maybe. I guess. But she was really good at letting guys down easy. Like just yesterday, I heard her on the phone, telling someone she couldn't see him anymore. She was really gentle about it."

"So then she did have a dispute recently," Dolan noted.

"Oh, yeah, I guess," Gabby said, seeming to realize only now that the call fit the profile Jessie had described.

"Who was she talking to?" Jessie asked quickly, not wanting the vibe to get too accusatory.

"I don't know. The other voice on the line was loud. But I was in a different room. I didn't want Claire to know I was listening in. Can't you guys trace that kind of thing?"

"Yes, we can, Gabby," Jessie said reassuringly. "What else can you tell us about last night?"

"I already told the other detectives about the date she had that night. She usually kept all the details in her phone."

"Is it possible that she brought her date back to the house, as you did with Carter?" Jessie asked.

"I doubt it," Gabby said, settling into the chaise a little more. She looked like she was fading a bit.

"Why not?" Jessie asked.

"She didn't like to bring guys back to our place. If she was feeling…friendly she'd usually go to theirs. She didn't like people knowing where she lived. She's had a few bad experiences, you know?"

"Actually," Dolan said, looking peeved, "we don't know. But it sounds like exactly the sort of think we'd want to pursue. Can you give us any names?"

"None jump to mind," Gabby said, oblivious to the fact that she was contradicting herself repeatedly. "I didn't really keep track of her dates unless she mentioned a name a few times. I figured that if it wasn't important enough to her, I didn't need to commit it to memory either."

Jessie got the sense that there were enough "dates" between the two of them that keeping track of names might be challenging. She looked over at Carter Harrington, who was shifting the weight on his feet back and forth uncomfortably, as if the conversation was getting into territory he'd rather avoid. She was debating whether this was the moment to go to those places when Dolan dived in.

32

"Ms. Cantu," he said, his tone dropping any pretense of warmth, "it's pretty clear you're hiding a few things from us. I don't know if you're aware of this, but lying to a federal agent is a crime."

Jessie's heart sank. The girl was already fragile, and threatening her seemed counterproductive

"I'm not lyi—" Gabby started to insist.

Dolan cut her off.

"Even saying you're not lying could be construed as a lie," he noted. "There is clearly something going on with your and Claire's dates that you are holding back on sharing with us. I get it. You don't want to incriminate yourself. But here's the thing, we're going to find everything out anyway, eventually. The only questions are: will it be sooner or later and will you be helpful or not. If it's sooner and you're helpful, we can be very accommodating. If it's later and you're not, we can be very tough."

Gabby looked terrified. Jessie tried to tamp things down a bit without stepping on Dolan's toes too much. She decided not to play good cop so much as less terrifying cop.

"Gabby, your help, right now, could be the difference between us catching whoever did this to Claire or not. Every second we're in the dark is another second her killer has to hide his involvement and cover his tracks. You don't want to be responsible for that, do you?"

She shook her head.

"And you don't want to face charges of obstructing a federal investigation either," Dolan added forcefully.

"No," Gabby whispered.

"Then let's have it," he demanded.

"We didn't break any laws," she insisted plaintively. "We just…date a lot of guys. Mostly older guys, sometimes married."

"Are you escorts?" Dolan asked, refusing to play nice.

"No!" she said adamantly. "We just let them buy us stuff. Every now and then, we hit the jackpot and one of them becomes a—have you ever heard the term 'sugar daddy'?"

"Yes," Dolan said, admirably keeping the condescension out of his voice this once.

"Well, that's what we're after," she said before turning to Harrington and adding, "no offense."

"Believe me," Jessie said, "none of this comes as a shock to him. He knew what he was signing up for. Go on."

"So when one of us found a sugar daddy, he'd usually agree to help pay for our rent and other stuff like that. Sometimes that might last a few weeks. Sometimes it would go on for months. We'd usually rotate guys in and out. But sometimes it would turn into something more. One of us would become sort of a professional mistress for a while. Eventually, we'd break it off when it got boring. It almost always got boring. Sometimes he'd end it, usually if he thought his wife might find out."

"How might his wife find out?" Jessie asked, sensing the answer. "And remember what Agent Dolan said about lying to the FBI."

"It's possible that me or Claire would tell a guy his wife should know the truth. Usually that would scare them off. Sometimes they'd even give us a little extra to make sure we kept quiet."

"That's called extortion," Dolan pointed out.

"It's what?" Gabby said, genuinely clueless.

"You didn't want to keep the relationship going?" Jessie asked quickly, not wanting to get tripped up on secondary issues. "Maybe hope the guy would leave his wife for you?"

"Are you kidding?" Gabby asked, sounding almost insulted. "I'm twenty-three. I'm not ready to settle down. This way I get all the perks but I can still party without being on someone's leash. The whole point of this is to have fun without having to work too hard for it. I mean, maybe I'll settle down when I get old, like twenty-six or something. But right now, I want to have a good time."

There was a long silence in the room. No one seemed to know how to react to that truth bomb. Jessie tried to wrap her head around the fact that in Gabby's mind, as a near-thirty-year-old, she was elderly.

"How did you find these guys?" she finally managed to ask.

"There's a website. It's called 'The Look of Love' or 'LOL' for short. It helps wealthy older guys meet up with friendly younger girls for dates. What happens after that is between them."

"Do you set up a profile on the site?" Jessie pressed.

"Yeah, that way the guys can find girls who are their type. And it lets the site do a security check on the guys."

Jessie and Dolan looked up at Harrington, who had retreated to the corner of the den and was looking out one of the massive windows facing Santa Monica.

"Did you go through one of those checks?" Dolan asked him.

Harrington turned around, sighed deeply, and walked back over to them.

"Yes," he admitted.

"You weren't worried about this website having you on file as a client?" Jessie wanted to know.

"I heard about it through a friend who vouched for it. He knows the person who runs the site, so there's some accountability. Plus, it's a pretty exclusive circle. There are maybe fifteen to twenty clients and less than a hundred girls. It's in everyone's interest to keep things under wraps."

"We'll need the name of the site operator," Jessie told him.

Harrington looked ashen.

"But like Gabby said," he balked, "there's nothing illegal about it. It's just a really exclusive dating service."

"We're not looking to shut it down," Jessie assured him, though the idea was appealing. "We just need to access Claire's profile and dating history."

"Would you mention that you got the information from me?" he whined.

"Only if we have to," Dolan said, showing what Jessie considered more deference to him than to Gabby.

"Don't worry," she added tartly. "You should be able to keep this hidden from your wife, at least until the trial."

"What?" he asked, genuinely horrified.

"Mr. Harrington," she said, knowing she was taking more pleasure in this than she probably should, "when we catch this guy, he's going to face trial. You'll have to testify in open court. So you'd be well-advised to figure out how you plan to explain your 'date' to Mrs. Harrington. Maybe you should call her before she returns from whatever extended trip she's currently on, the one that has you so comfortable parading Gabrielle around. I wish you luck."

CHAPTER SIX

Jessie was flabbergasted.

"Can you repeat that?" she asked incredulously.

"You heard me," Dolan said as they stood in the driveway outside the front of Harrington's mansion. "Now that the case is closed, I'm headed back to the station."

"The case is *not* closed," she reminded him. "There's a murderer with blood-soaked keys out there somewhere."

"That's not my concern," Dolan said nonchalantly. "The case is closed in terms of Crutchfield and Thurman. It's clear that whoever did this, it wasn't one of them. And since I'm after those two, this case is officially in the rearview mirror. Besides, the North Hollywood detectives can handle this just fine. They can just get names from the dating site and find out which of them don't have alibis. I bet this thing is solved in twelve hours, without any help from us."

Jessie knew he was right. The original detectives, whom she hadn't even met, were probably more than capable of working this case. And there no longer seemed to be any connection to either of the serial killers she was associated with. That made it hard to justify continuing to pursue the killer.

But she really wanted to. Not all her reasons were altruistic. One was simply the thrill of the chase. Having been stashed away at the WITSEC house for days now, she'd been unable to scratch that itch. Now that she'd gotten a taste for the hunt, she couldn't just shut that instinct down.

She also knew that if Captain Decker agreed with Dolan that this case had no connection to either serial killer, her vaunted inside knowledge and forensic skills would be rendered moot. She was only allowed to pursue this case in the first place because it seemed like one where she might have special insight into the killer. If that was no longer true, then there was no reason for her to be there. And that likely meant she'd be sent back to that boring house in Palms and expected to spend endless, soul-draining hours by the pool. Anything that could prevent that outcome was worth pursuing.

Finally, independent of her own situation, there was the girl. She'd seen Claire's face, so young and beautiful, frozen in a mask of fear. She'd seen the ugly perforations that had turned her neck into a pulpy mess. Just because she wasn't the victim of a serial killer didn't mean that Claire Stanton wasn't entitled to justice too. If Jessie could help make that happen, she had an obligation to do so. She couldn't just pass the case off if it wasn't convenient for her. So she lied.

"We don't know this isn't the work of Crutchfield or Thurman yet," she finally said, making even Murph and Toomey turn around in surprise.

"What are you talking about?" Dolan asked incredulously. "This killing has none of the signs of either one of them."

"None of the *obvious* signs," she said with impressive conviction. "But both of these men are smart. They'd know that using their standard methods would be a dead giveaway. Using keys as the murder weapon would allow either of them to satisfy that murderous urge without revealing their involvement. It would actually be a clever move to throw off suspicion, which seems to be working with you right now."

Dolan stared at her with a mix of bemusement, frustration, and a hint of admiration.

"Are you really trying to sell me on the idea that Thurman or Crutchfield, while being hunted, and in one case, badly injured, took the time to travel to the San Fernando Valley and murder some random party girl with a weapon neither has ever used before?"

Jessie smiled politely at his tirade, knowing it would only infuriate him more.

"I don't have to sell you on the idea, Agent Dolan. I just have to sell my captain. You're more than welcome to drop the case and I'll continue to pursue it on my own. As you noted, there are two dangerous killers on the loose, and I for one intend to leave no stone unturned in the search for them. But you do you."

"You are a real piece of work," Dolan said.

Jessie smiled sweetly as she opened the car door and got in.

"So I've been told."

*

It didn't take long for Jessie's confidence to crumble.

Back at the station, as she waited to make her pitch to Captain Decker, something was going on. No one said anything overt but she could sense a heightened energy in the air.

She wondered if a more credible lead in the hunt for either man had emerged, making her questionable argument for staying on the Stanton case unconvincing. If that was the case, she didn't have a backup plan. Whatever was going on, it was big. She was ushered into the same isolated conference room, where she waited with Murph for twenty uneventful minutes. Dolan had disappeared.

"Do you know what's going on?" she asked Murph.

He looked at her, mildly satisfied with her discomfort.

"How would I know anything?" he asked. "I've been stuck in here with you."

"You've got that earpiece," she pointed out. "I'm sure you're getting updates."

"Can't help you," he replied, seemingly enjoying being in a more commanding position after several hours of being a glorified personal driver. Before she could respond, the door opened and both Decker and Dolan walked in.

"There's been a development," the captain said without preamble.

Jessie could tell immediately that whatever the news was, it wasn't good. Decker's already deeply lined face was even more creased than usual and he seemed reluctant to make eye contact. Somehow she knew the news was connected to her. Decker seemed hesitant to go on. Behind him, Dolan looked even more taciturn than usual.

"Go ahead, Captain," she said, steeling herself. "I can take it."

"Ernie Cortez has been found."

That should have been great news. Ernie was the NRD security officer who killed his co-workers and helped Bolton Crutchfield escape. If he'd been located, they might finally have a lead on Crutchfield's location. But the demeanor of both men suggested she ought not get too excited.

"I'm sensing there's more," she said.

"He's dead," Decker sighed.

"Heart attack?" Jessie asked skeptically, trying to keep the creeping panic she felt at bay.

Dolan stepped forward.

"He was found in an alley dumpster about six blocks from here. The man was gutted from sternum to pelvis. His insides were lying next to the dumpster. That's how they managed to find him."

Jessie leaned back in her chair, trying to process the news. Crutchfield had secretly cultivated Ernie for years, essentially seducing him. It had worked so well that Ernie had willingly slaughtered a half dozen of his own co-workers in the service of a serial killer. And now Crutchfield had brutally, unceremoniously dispensed with him.

Why? Had Ernie disappointed or angered him in some way? Had he turned on his master?

But she knew that couldn't be the main reason. If it was, he wouldn't have left the body so close to the place where he knew Jessie worked. It was a message—for her.

"What are you leaving out? What's the part you're afraid to tell me?"

The two men looked at each other. In the corner of the room, Murph conspicuously studied his shoes.

"He left a note," Decker finally said. "It was folded into a tiny square and placed in a small plastic bag, which was nailed to the roof of Cortez's mouth. The note was addressed to you."

"Of course it was," Jessie said, more resigned than shocked. "Do you have it with you?"

"It's with forensics right now. But we scanned it."

"May I see it?" Jessie asked.

Decker nodded and pulled up the image on his phone, then handed it to her. She immediately recognized Crutchfield's handwriting, a realization she didn't know what to make of. The note was shorter and more straightforward than she'd expected, with only a bit of the flowery language the man usually used. It read:

Miss Jessie,

I hope this correspondence finds you well. I apologize for the method of delivery. I know you were fond of Ernie, though I suspect that affection has abated of late. I thought you might want to know that I recently had a get-together with your father. He was...concerned that my loyalty to him may have been compromised by my time with you. What a charge! But he is moving past that. I anticipate that soon he'll be recovered enough from his injuries to

attempt another reunion with you. Expect to see him presently. It should be a killer meeting. May the strongest Thurman prevail!
  Respectfully,
  Bolton

Jessie looked up to see the three men in the room staring at her, waiting for her reaction. She knew that any hint of apprehension would reinforce their collective inclination to return her to the safe house immediately. So she stifled it.

"If he wasn't a brutal killer, I'd say the guy had a future writing for Hallmark. He really has a way with words, don't you think?"

"It's okay to be unsettled," Decker replied, ignoring her bravado. "I'm unsettled by it."

"I'm not unsettled," Jessie insisted, unsure how convincing she was. "If anyone understands how these guys operate, it's me. I have two serial killers fixated on me, one of whom is my own father. If I had let that affect me, I'd be curled up in a ball by now. I actually view this as a good thing."

"How's that?" Dolan challenged.

Yes, how is that, Jessie?

"First of all, Ernie's off the board now. That's one less psycho I have to worry about. Second, in his weird way, I think this is Crutchfield helping me. He's trying to warn me that my father is almost ready to come after me again."

"It's not clear to me that he's picked a side in that fight," Decker countered.

"I'm not saying he's picked a side," Jessie said. "I just think he wants a fair fight. And he believes that letting me know Xander Thurman is almost back to hunting and killing strength makes it fairer."

Dolan stepped forward, a dubious expression his face.

"How do you know he's not just trying to manipulate you, to lure you into a false sense of security in order to draw you out into the open?"

Jessie almost snorted her incredulity.

"In what world does slicing a man open, pouring his innards into an alley, and hammering a note into the body's mouth with a nail give me a false sense of security? I know who I'm dealing with here."

40

"So do I," Decker interjected, "which is why, now that we're sure this Valley case is unrelated, I'm sending you back to the safe house."

Jessie's heart sank. This was what she'd feared. But she barely let a second pass before responding.

"No way," she retorted. "Now that I know the waiting game is over, there is not a chance in hell that I'm going back to some ranch house in Palms to wait to be attacked."

Murph stirred at that.

"You make it sound like they're just waiting to descend on the place," he said. "Neither of those men has a clue about that house. That's why the body was dropped near here. This is the only location Crutchfield can connect to you, which is why the Service didn't want you to come. But now that you have, we plan to secrete you back at the house and keep you there until this is resolved."

Jessie could feel the energy in the room working against her. Unless something changed fast, she was going to lose this fight. Then, from the least likely source she could have imagined, came a lifeline.

"Or we could try something else."

Everyone looked over at the speaker. It was Dolan.

CHAPTER SEVEN

Jessie's mouth dropped open.

She saw Captain Decker's do the same. This crusty FBI agent was about ten seconds from parting ways with her for good. That he would do anything to undermine that was a shock.

"Come again?" Murph said, equally stunned.

"I actually can't believe I'm about to say this myself, but hear me out," Dolan said. "Maybe the best way to keep Ms. Hunt safe is to keep her on the move."

"What are you talking about?" Decker asked, trying to rein in his hostility to the idea.

"Look, Hunt could still go back the safe house at night. But now that we know the Stanton case has nothing to do with either Crutchfield or Thurman, maybe we should stick with it. Following up leads and interviewing witnesses—all of that will have her in unexpected places at unpredictable times. Her whereabouts will be virtually impossible to track. And the whole time, she'd have an FBI agent and a small army of US marshals by her side."

Decker and Murph both looked unconvinced but neither spoke. Dolan took advantage of their silence to press harder.

"Look, Captain," he continued. "I'm sure you have full confidence in everyone in your precinct. And Marshal Murphy—I know you feel the same way. But if Ernie Cortez was compromised, someone else on the inside might be too. But if we're constantly on the move and even *we* don't know where we're going next, that makes it pretty hard for an accomplice to tip off Crutchfield or Thurman. It just means fewer holes to plug."

"Right," Jessie chimed in. "And after a day of constant movement, I'd go back to the safe house, more confident in my security and actually feeling like I made a difference that day."

"And no one would even know when that would happen," Dolan piggybacked. "When we part ways tonight, I won't know where she's going. I assume you don't know the location of the safe house other than that it's in Palms, Captain?"

Decker shook his head. Dolan turned to Jessie at that point.

"By the way," he added snarkily, "maybe don't go announcing the neighborhood of your safe house to anyone who's not supposed to know it. Just a security tip."

Jessie felt the urge to punch him square in the nose, but forced it down. After all, he was the main reason she might actually not be politely imprisoned in the next hour.

"Thanks, Agent," she said saccharinely before turning to Captain Decker. "So what do you think?"

Decker, in turn, looked at Murph, who she now knew was professionally called Marshal Murphy.

"I'm still opposed," he said, though not as adamantly as she had expected. "It's against procedure and it puts the protectee at unnecessary risk."

She noted that he didn't officially shut down the idea, however. Maybe he didn't have the authority to overrule her superior officer.

Decker leaned forward, his arms resting on the conference table, lost in thought. No one spoke. Finally, after what had to be at least twenty seconds, he lifted his head.

*

They turned the conference room into a makeshift office.

Phones were brought in so they could make calls. Each of them was issued a clean laptop for temporary use. Murph reluctantly brought in a third chair now that it was clear they wouldn't be leaving anytime soon. Poor Toomey was left to sit in his car in the garage.

The third marshal, a smallish forty-something guy named Collica with the sinewy build of an ultra-marathoner, was assigned to sit in the precinct waiting room and eyeball everyone who entered. The fourth member of her protective detail, a tall, barrel-chested, buzzcut-blond named Emerson, circled the block, parking intermittently. Occasionally he and Collica switched positions.

In the brief window while their equipment was being set up, Jessie asked Dolan to join her alone in the hallway. But Murph stopped them, saying he'd go outside instead. As soon as the door closed behind him, Jessie asked the question on her mind.

"Why did you back me up in there?"

"You didn't want me to?" he asked. "I figured you'd be happy I did. You were seconds from being shut down."

"I am happy," she said, noting that he'd completely avoided the question. "But I want to know why. A few hours ago, you were ready to be done with this case and with me. You could have been back at your office by now. I seriously doubt you fought for this because of your deep respect for me. So why?"

"It's not that complicated," he insisted, shrugging. "I was serious about how moving around probably keeps you safer. And you seemed to care about this girl. I figured you deserved a chance to get justice for her. Does there have to be more to it than that?"

"Yes, because I don't think you give a damn about either of those things. Besides, even if that's true, you didn't have to stick around. Hell, you strong-armed that case away from the detectives in North Hollywood Division even though this is hardly an FBI matter."

"You might be surprised at what I care about," he said, sounding genuinely hurt. "I'll admit that staying around here at Central Station probably keeps me closer to developments in the search for these serial killers. But I don't like to see young girls murdered either. There's no reason I can't work this case with you and keep my ears open around here."

Jessie still didn't buy it. But she wasn't inclined to push too hard at the moment. After all, she was on the case, able to move around rather than stay cooped up in that house. Rather than be a potential victim, she was in pursuer mode. That's the way she preferred it.

When everything was set up, they got to work. Dolan checked out Claire's phone records while Jessie tried to get access to her dating site account. She was getting pushback.

"We value our clients' privacy," the British-accented woman on the phone said officiously over the speakerphone after hearing the situation.

"Even when it comes to a murder?" Jessie asked incredulously.

"No matter what the situation," the woman replied with off-putting coldness.

Jessie looked down at her notes and found the name Carter Harrington had given her for the person who ran the company.

"Let me speak to Kane Sanders," she said.

"I can pass along your message, but Kane is unavailable right now."

Jessie felt the blood in her veins pump a little faster. She struggled to keep her voice even as she responded.

"Kane should know that the LAPD doesn't appreciate being jerked around and that there may be a warrant in the near future to search the offices of the Look of Love website if you can't be more accommodating."

"And *you* should know," the woman replied in the same obnoxious tone as before, "that Kane has a legal team that will quickly dispense with any such warrant. Also, you should know that harassment isn't a great look on you."

All of a sudden Jessie noticed Dolan standing over her.

"May I?" he asked, pointing at the phone.

Jessie nodded.

"Ma'am," he said loudly, "this is agent Jack Dolan with the FBI. What's your name?"

"My name is Darian," the woman said, sounding slightly less sure of herself than before.

"Are you certain of that, ma'am?" Dolan asked. "Because, as you may or may not be aware, lying to a federal agent is a crime."

"How dare you assert that—"

"Don't waste my time," Dolan interrupted, completely unfazed. "I think we both know that Kane is more than available. So stop screwing around."

After a long pause, Darian replied.

"Hold for a moment, please."

There were fifteen seconds of Muzak, after which another female voice came on the line.

"This is Kane Sanders. How may I help you?"

Jessie looked up at Dolan, who was smiling. She realized what he must have known all along. Kane *was* Darian, sans the crappy accent.

"Hi, Kane," he replied, making no mention of what he knew. "Thanks for making the time. Here's the deal. As I'm sure Darian informed you, I'm an FBI agent. My partner and I are investigating the death of a young woman who used your site. You're going to give us full access to all your data today."

"Why on Earth would I do that?" she demanded.

"Because if you don't, me and some reporters from a few of my favorite local news stations will be outside your address for a press conference that will detail all the sordid particulars of how the Look of Love dating site works. We'll wrap up just in time for the six o'clock news. Or, if you prefer, you can give us the information we need and I can postpone the press conference. How would you like to proceed, Darian, er, I mean Kane?"

There were several moments of silence. When Kane responded she sounded a little bit broken.

"Do you have a pen?" she asked.

"I do," Dolan replied gleefully.

"Here's her login information."

"Nope," he said. "I need administrator access."

"But that would reveal the real names of our clients," she protested.

"I'm not looking to shut you down, Kane," he assured her with something close to sympathy. "My understanding is that your business, while reprehensible, isn't illegal. I don't intend to arrest anyone for simply using it, only for murdering Claire Stanton."

"Do I have your word?" Kane pleaded.

"Sure," Dolan said. "It's not worth much. But if that's what gets you over the hump, I give you my solemn word."

As Kane dictated the login information and Jessie wrote it down, Dolan walked out of the conference room into the hall, where his laughing was less likely to be heard.

CHAPTER EIGHT

The website was a treasure trove.

It was full of salacious material on the predilections of their clients, many of whose names Jessie recognized. They included a well-known criminal defense attorney, several CEOs, a prominent local politician, and multiple major Hollywood players, including some executives, a couple of directors, and one extremely well-known movie star. According to the site data, Claire had been involved with almost a dozen of them over the last two years.

The website's setup was actually quite clever. Almost all communication after initially signing up was done through the associated app. That way messaging was maintained in one discreet location, surely a selling point for these high-profile men. Even within the messaging portion of the app, clients and their potential dates were identified by numbers rather than names. It was a pretty impressive, secure operation. That is, unless it ran up against a pushy FBI agent.

The message exchange that showed the most promise to Jessie was one from member #401B22, who happened to be West Hollywood City Councilman Milton Jerebko. It was from two days ago.

In it, Claire—member 62W3—had overtly threatened to go public with their relationship. The reason wasn't clear. But it had evoked a strong reaction from Jerebko. After a testy back and forth, his final message read: *Do this and I will end you.* That seemed worth checking out.

After checking with Jerebko's office and learning that he was working from home that day, the group, or Four Musketeers as Dolan had taken to calling them, piled in the Marshals Service sedan. The drive to Jerebko's house in the hills above West Hollywood took over a half hour, allowing Dolan to fill Jessie in on what he'd learned from Claire's phone records, which was: not much.

"She texted all the time but almost never made calls," he noted. "And the ones she did make were mostly for retail services. She almost never actually talked to anyone."

"Kids these days," Jessie said in her best old man voice.

"There are several calls to and from pay phones in the last few weeks," he continued, pretending not to hear her. "That seems odd for such a modern girl."

"The same pay phone every time?" Jessie asked, suddenly interested.

"No. Each call is at a different location. But they're all in the same general area, this side of the hills, along the corridor from Hollywood west to Beverly Hills."

"Just the area that our friendly neighborhood councilman would be traveling in," Jessie noted.

"True," Dolan acknowledged, "but it seems odd that they would communicate that way when they were already being so direct over the app."

"Maybe they had agreed to financial terms and he wanted an extra layer of security for that chat," Jessie surmised.

"Or it could be something completely unrelated," Dolan replied. "Maybe Claire bought her drugs from a dealer who liked to stay on the move."

"So your theory is that out of nowhere, Claire became an addict who coordinated her pickups over a pay phone."

"Addiction can happen fast," Dolan countered.

Jessie was skeptical but not in the mood to argue about it.

"I guess the preliminary toxicology report will help with that," she said. "We should have it later today."

From the front seat, Jessie heard a soft grunt from Murph. Dolan clearly heard it too.

"You have thoughts on the matter, Marshal Murphy?" he asked.

"Not my area," Murph replied.

"And yet, you have thoughts. I'd love to hear them."

Murph sat still for a moment, seemingly debating whether to engage. Jessie could tell that he was itching to. A second later he did.

"I'm not an investigator but I doubt she's an addict. The pictures in her room, even late-night party ones, never showed her looking cloudy-eyed or out of control. She had medals for multiple endurance races framed on her wall and a bib from the LA Marathon

48

on her dresser. That was only a few weeks ago. It's hard to imagine that she suddenly did a deep dive into drugs at the same time she was training for and completing a twenty-six-mile race. I guess anything is possible. But she didn't strike me as the type."

Both Jessie and Dolan sat in the backseat quietly, pondering what he'd said. Jessie silently chastised herself for not noticing all the running-related paraphernalia in the house. It was a reminder that she still had a lot to learn on this job.

The drive up to Jerebko's house was an adventure. The roads leading into the Hollywood Hills were narrow, with cars parked on both sides. Often only one car could pass by at a time. And they were winding, with corkscrews and switchbacks that had Jessie borderline nauseated by the time they pulled up to the house.

"This place seems pretty extraordinary for a public servant," Dolan noted.

Three stories high and consuming half a block, the whole property was surrounded by a ten-foot-tall stone wall. Jessie had done some preliminary research on the family and knew that it wasn't purchased on a councilman's salary.

"Actually, his wife bought it," she said. "Gayle Martindale Jerebko is a descendant of the wealthy Martindales, who originally struck it rich in the California Gold Rush of 1849. Most of the clan still lives in San Francisco. But while at Stanford, Gayle fell in love with a scrappy young student activist named Milton Jerebko. When he moved to Southern California, she followed."

"A woman from that background threw in her lot with a political activist?" Dolan asked incredulously.

"There's no telling when it comes to love, Dolan. Also, I guess she saw potential in him," Jessie replied. "Turns out she had good reason. Milton eventually entered politics after gaining popularity with the local community for his vocal support of healthcare for homeless gay youth. He swept to victory in his city council race six years ago and was rumored to be considering running for mayor of West Hollywood or maybe even Los Angeles itself. After he was elected to the council, Gayle took over leadership of their healthcare foundation. According to news reports, she's known as a tireless fundraiser for the cause. Neither has ever been arrested."

"Family?" Dolan wanted to know.

"They have two children in high school, a daughter entering her senior year and a son about to become a sophomore. The only brush with the law for any of them was when their daughter accidentally rear-ended another driver while taking her driver's test."

They seemed like the perfect couple, which made Jessie inherently suspicious. As she reviewed what she knew about the Jerebkos in her head, the four of them got out of the car and walked to the main gate, passing the other Marshal vehicle idling across the street. Dolan was about to hit the buzzer when a voice came over the speaker.

"Please state your business," a clipped male voice said.

"At least we know it's not Darian," Jessie muttered under her breath.

Dolan forced back a smile as he responded.

"I'm Special Agent Jack Dolan of the FBI," he said. "We need to speak to Councilman Jerebko."

"May I see your identification, Agent?" the voice asked. "Please hold it up to the camera to your left."

Dolan did as he was asked. After a moment, the voice continued.

"To what is this pertaining?"

"A matter that can only be discussed with the councilman. Please open the gate now."

There was another pause, followed by a bell. The gate began to slowly grind open.

"Please proceed to the main entrance at the top of the driveway," the voice said. "You will be met at the door."

They did just that, traversing the steep cobblestone path to the imposing front door. On the way up, Jessie leaned over to Murph.

"You know, now that I'm back in the field, I think it might be advisable to return my service weapon. I feel a bit naked without it."

Murph looked briefly conflicted before replying.

"It's back at the safe house. I'll have it taken to the station. Do you think you can question this middle-aged couple without it? Or should I call for more backup?"

Jessie considered a quippy comeback but still hadn't come up with one when the front door opened. Jessie was mildly surprised not to see an elderly man in a butler's suit. Instead it was a twenty-something guy in slacks and a button-down shirt.

"Hello, I'm Elias, the Jerebko family's house manager. Are you all with the FBI?" he asked, trying to hide his obvious apprehension.

"They're US Marshals. She's LAPD," Dolan said. "It's a multi-jurisdictional unit."

"I'll need to see everyone's identification," Elias insisted.

Murph and Toomey pulled theirs out and shoved them in Elias's face. Jessie was just about to show hers too when Murph grabbed her wrist and pulled her hand down.

"Enough of this," he said impatiently. "This is a time-sensitive matter. We can give you our birth certificates later if you like. But we need to speak to the councilman now."

"But she..." Elias started, nodding at Jessie.

"And don't go anywhere," Dolan added, interrupting him. "We may have questions for you later."

Elias backed down and motioned for them to follow him. As he led them through the massive foyer and an ornate hallway, Jessie glanced first at Murph and then at Dolan. It didn't escape her attention that the two of them had worked in concert to ensure that Elias never actually saw her ID, and therefore her name. Clearly everyone was serious about keeping her whereabouts as secret as possible.

It took a good minute to reach what Elias referred to as "the back den," where the Jerebkos were waiting for them. They both stood up when the group entered. Beyond his age, somewhere in the mid-forties—Milton Jerebko was nothing like Jessie had predicted he would be. He wasn't exactly good-looking. But he made the most of what he had.

Tall and muscular, he had a tanned face and his slightly thinning dark hair was groomed to perfection. His suit jacket rested casually on the arm of the couch beside him and he wore navy slacks and a bold pink dress shirt with his sky-blue tie slightly loosened. He had a broad smile and exuded confidence as he extended his hand to Jessie first and then the others as he introduced himself.

"I'm Milt," he said in a booming voice. "This is my wife, Gayle."

Gayle shook all their hands as well. Also in her forties, she was as immaculate as her husband. Blonde and statuesque with a figure that suggested hours of hard work at the gym, she looked like she could have been Claire's mother. Jessie forced that uncomfortable thought from her head.

"To what do we owe the honor of the entire Los Angeles law enforcement community?" Jerebko asked after all the handshakes hand concluded.

"Well, Councilman," Dolan began, "it might be better if we discussed this matter with you privately."

Jessie noted that he used the man's formal title rather than just his name, a subtle reminder that the stakes were higher than usual for a public official. But it didn't seem to faze Jerebko—at least not yet.

"Anything you have to discuss with me, you can discuss in front of my wife," he said confidently.

Jessie suspected he might regret being so blustery.

"All right," she said, deciding to test the theory. "We're here about Claire Stanton."

"Ah, of course," he said expectantly. "I had a feeling that might be what this was about. How many other folks has she tried to extort?"

"Excuse me?" Jessie asked, genuinely surprised.

"I'm assuming you're doing some kind of investigation into her attempts to extort folks she's been involved with. I can't be the only one."

Jessie stared at him in stunned silence. Dolan stepped into the void.

"Are you acknowledging that you had a relationship with Ms. Stanton?"

"I wouldn't really call it a relationship. But we were involved, yes. That is, until she tried to pressure me to pay her to stay quiet."

Jessie looked over at Gayle Jerebko, whose tight expression was somewhere between a smile and a grimace. Clearly, she was not loving this.

"You were aware of this relationship?" Jessie asked her.

"I was made aware of it recently," she said tersely. "After this woman tried to blackmail Milt, he came clean to me rather than pay."

"And how has that been for you?" Jessie couldn't help but ask, even though it wasn't strictly professional.

"I can't say that the last few days have been the greatest of my life. First, learning your husband has been unfaithful. Then finding out his mistress is trying to extort him. But it was the right course of action. Paying would have just made things worse. This way, her threats have no power."

"What about with the voters?" Jessie countered. "Even if you don't hold this against him, they might."

"My constituents are very understanding," Jerebko said, shifting effortlessly into politician mode. "This is a pretty forgiving community. In my experience, as long as you are doing the work of the people, folks around here don't get too exercised about personal peccadilloes. I had been toying with the idea of a press conference to get everything out in the open. Now that it looks like law enforcement is involved, I'm even more certain that I should. It will be hard on Gayle and the kids, who did nothing to bring this about. But it's the right thing to do. How long do I have? Has she been arrested?"

"No, she hasn't," Dolan said flatly.

"Why not?" Jerebko asked.

"Because she was murdered."

CHAPTER NINE

Jessie knew it was coming.

The way Dolan set it up, she could tell ahead of time that he was about to drop the bomb. She wondered if he'd done that deliberately so that she could prepare herself to watch the couple's reactions. If so, it worked. When the words came out of his mouth, her eyes were fixed on the Jerebkos.

Both of them looked legitimately stunned. But there was more. In Milton's case, she saw the wheels turn almost immediately, as he processed the fact that he was almost certainly a suspect. Gayle's shock seemed intermingled with something close to satisfaction, perhaps at the fact that the woman who had upended her life was no longer drawing breath. Both reactions were unflattering. But neither necessarily indicated any guilt.

"How?" Milton finally managed to gasp.

"For obvious reasons, we can't really get into the details at this time," Dolan said. "But we are going to need statements from both of you regarding your whereabouts last night."

"You're suggesting we had a hand in this?" Gayle asked, her back growing stiff.

"It's not an outrageous possibility," Dolan said. "Especially in light of what you've told us...and what you haven't."

"What is that supposed to mean?" Milton spat, his charm fading fast.

"Well, Councilman, you neglected to mention your threat toward Ms. Stanton over a dating app."

"Dating app?" Gayle repeated, perplexed. "You met this woman on an *app*?"

Milton's expression went from self-righteous to sheepish in an instant.

"Whoa, it looks like you two still have a bit to discuss," Dolan said, chuckling to himself before turning suddenly serious. "In the meantime, care to address the threat, sir?"

"What threat?"

"The threat to 'end her' if she went public about your indiscretion."

"Oh, Jesus," Jerebko groaned. "That's not what it seems like. I meant end her financially. My lawyers were going to sue her into the ground—defamation, fraud, anything they could come up with. I'd never actually hurt someone physically."

"Do you have any proof that this was a legal and not a physical threat?" Jessie asked.

"I talked to my lawyers the same day she messaged me. I'll waive attorney-client privilege if it will help prove that."

"One doesn't preclude the other," Dolan said.

"What?"

"Threatening her legally doesn't preclude you from going after her physically," he said.

"Oh my god," Jerebko said, looking truly flustered.

"Where were you last night, Mr. Jerebko?" Jessie asked, hoping to get a more honest answer now, when he was less composed.

"I was in San Diego. I just drove back this morning."

"We'll have to verify that," Jessie said before turning to Gayle. "Where were you, ma'am?"

"I was here," she said, still looking somewhat dazed at the sudden turn of events. "I played board games with my kids, then went to bed."

"You play board games with your kids?" Murph asked, speaking for the first time. Dolan shot him an annoyed look.

"Yes," she answered. "Trivial Pursuit, Scattergories. We have 'no media' nights where we just hang out—no phones, no TV, just live, personal interaction."

"And your kids will vouch for that?" Jessie asked, wanting to get away from the humanity of the suspects and keep them on the defensive.

"If they have to," Gayle replied. "I'd rather protect them from this if possible. Maybe you can check my phone GPS or something instead? But if you require it, then yes, they can vouch for my whereabouts."

"And what about you, Councilman?" Dolan asked, turning his attention back to Milton. "Who in San Diego can vouch for you?"

"I don't know," Jerebko said uncertainly. "I went there for a conference in the afternoon. But I didn't see many people after that."

"Maybe at the hotel you stayed at? Perhaps the front desk agent who checked you in?"

"It was pretty crowded," he said unconvincingly. "I doubt he'd remember me."

"All right," Dolan pressed. "Then just give us the hotel name and we'll check it out for you."

"I don't recall it offhand," Jerebko replied. "But I can get it for you."

"You don't have a receipt, Councilman?" Dolan asked skeptically.

Jerebko looked at him angrily.

"Why do keep saying 'councilman' like it's a bad word?" he demanded.

"I'm just trying to get to the bottom of things, sir," Dolan said calmly.

Of course Jessie knew that wasn't the case. As she'd suspected, he was using the title because it reminded Jerebko that he held the public's trust and that in some way, either large or small, he had broken it. He knew that would eat at the guy and possibly force him into a mistake of some kind. It finally seemed to be working.

"I think it's time you left," Jerebko said, seeming to regain some of his authority.

"I think it's time you came with us," Dolan replied quietly, quickly undermining it again. "You can do that as a respected public official, quietly and voluntarily coming into the station to help out with an ongoing investigation. Or we can do it more formally. I can read your rights and take you into custody. You can request a lawyer. Of course, the media might somehow find out about all this and stake us out as we brought you through the front door of the police station. That would be unfortunate. It's your call, Mr. Jerebko."

The man stood there, weighing his choice. As he did, Dolan added something that surprised Jessie.

"A bit of advice," he said quietly. "If what you're hiding is anything less than murder, you're better off coming in of your own accord. Whatever it is, we can probably work it out. If you killed her, you may as well let me arrest you and call your lawyer once we get there."

Jerebko looked at him with the most hangdog expression Jessie had seen in a long time. Then, in almost a whisper, he replied.

"Can I go to the bathroom first?" he asked pathetically.

*

Navigating the station was tricky.

While Dolan took Jerebko to the conference room for an informal, voluntary, not-yet-arrested interview, Murph made sure the coast was clear for Jessie to get through the halls without being seen by anyone who might blab about her presence.

She got the go-ahead. As she walked quickly to the conference room, Jessie couldn't shake the generalized feeling that even here she was unsafe. After all, Central Station was the one place that both Crutchfield and her father knew to look for her.

She doubted that either could access the facility—the security precautions were impressive even before she got formal Marshal Service protection. But even with all the safety measures the marshals were taking, all it would take was a single slip-up for one or both of them to find out she was here and follow her to her next location.

Frank Corcoran, the supervising agent, had assured her that multiple layers of protection had been put in place around the station which she had been intentionally kept unaware of. He warned that she might somehow inadvertently reveal their procedures with a glance or misplaced word. She found the suggestion borderline insulting but held her tongue, choosing not to fight that battle.

Part of her wondered if the marshals were intentionally putting her at risk, to use her as bait to draw out either killer. Then again, she had to admit that *she* was the one who'd insisted on coming to the station in the first place, not them.

When she finally entered the conference room, with Murph right behind her, Jerebko was sitting forlornly on a metal folding chair at the small card table in the center of the room. Dolan stood in the corner, scrolling through his phone. She took a long, deep breath and mentally pushed thoughts of any killers except Claire's from her mind.

"Glad you could join us," Dolan said when she walked in. "I was worried you got lost."

She didn't respond, not wanting to give Jerebko a hint that there was any animosity between his interrogators. Instead she sat down in a folding chair across from Jerebko and stared at him. He looked everywhere but at her.

"Mr. Jerebko," she finally said, taking the initiative before anyone else did, "I'm not a detective. I'm a criminal profiler. And my profile of you suggests that you were not being forthright about your time in San Diego. But to be honest, a pre-school teacher could have discerned the same thing. Your attempts to come up with an alibi would embarrass a three-year-old. So now that it's just us here, without your disappointed wife, why don't you save us all some time and come clean?"

She glanced at Dolan, who was now standing behind the councilman. He didn't say anything but his half-smile suggested he approved of her tactic. And with good reason, it turned out. Seconds later, Jerebko was spilling his guts.

"I was in San Diego yesterday," he insisted before admitting, "but I didn't spend the night there."

"Where were you?" she asked, keeping all judgment out of her voice.

"I paid for the room for the night but left and drove back to LA to meet someone."

"Who was that?" Jessie asked, trying to stay patient as she pulled the details out of him.

"I had another date with a different girl from the site."

"You weren't worried about additional blackmail threats?"

"A little. But the truth is, I was…lonely. Things were over with Claire and, as you can imagine, Gayle wasn't going to be in an amorous mood. So I made a date."

"We'll need her name," Jessie said.

"Of course," he agreed. "I can give you her name, her member number, whatever you need. I spent the night at her place, where, by the way, she didn't try to wring any money out of me."

"How nice that you found someone who really appreciates you for you, sir," Jessie said, unable to keep the sarcasm at bay.

"We'll need to keep you here while we follow this up," Dolan said quickly, now in the rare position of playing peacemaker.

"Whatever it takes," Jerebko said plaintively.

They left him in the conference room with an officer standing guard over him and the three of them—Jessie, Dolan, and Murph—moved to a nearby supply closet, the only place nearby without constant foot traffic, to talk. Murph spoke before either of them could.

"Ms. Hunt, you have a call. Normally, I wouldn't patch it through. But since it's coming in through the station switchboard and your captain authorized it, I'm willing to let you take it, as long as you don't reveal anything about your movements."

"Okay," Jessie said, her curiosity trumping her apprehension. "Who is it?"

"A Detective Ryan Hernandez."

Despite her best efforts, Jessie felt her cheeks flush.

CHAPTER TEN

"Oh. Okay," she said, trying to sound unruffled. "Where should I take it?"

"Take it here," Dolan said, clearly noting her suddenly pink face but saying nothing about it. "I'll check on Jerebko's alibi. And I'll follow up on his wife's phone data too. Find me when you're done."

She nodded. Murph spoke into his phone.

"Patch him through," he said, then handed it to her. "Not too long, okay? Even under secure conditions, this is a risk."

"Thanks," she said, taking the phone.

"I'll be right outside," he reminded her.

When he closed the door, she held the receiver up to her ear.

"Hello," she said hesitantly.

"Jessie," came the familiar voice of Ryan Hernandez, her friend, occasional case partner, and apparently now also the guy whose name made her blush involuntarily. "How are you?"

"I'm getting by," she said, glad her voice wasn't as out of control as her skin. "You know, solving cases, evading serial killers, that kind of thing."

"Just a typical day at the office for you, right?" he asked playfully.

"Sometime it feels like that."

"Well, I'm really sorry I haven't been in touch of late. I know I promised to keep you updated on hospitals that your psycho father might have gone to for treatment."

"That's okay," she said, though it wasn't. "The captain has kept me looped in. Besides, he told me you were helping on a triple homicide in Topanga Canyon so I know you've been busy."

"You think that's why I've been out of touch?" he asked, sounding slightly offended. "That's not it at all. I wouldn't let something like a few murders stop me from contacting you."

"What then?" she asked, surprised at his directness.

"Decker ordered me not to. He said that any kind of communication could put your security at risk. He said that, until

60

Crutchfield and Thurman are caught, he wanted you completely off the grid."

Jessie couldn't help but feel relieved. Even though she knew it was ridiculous, some primal part of her had started to wonder whether he'd just forgotten about her. At the same time she was immediately pissed at Captain Decker for doing that and not even telling her. She planned to have a discussion with him on that matter when things settled down.

"Why the call now then?"

"I heard about Ernie Cortez's murder and the note from Crutchfield," he said. "I figured you had to be bouncing off the walls. So I said 'screw it.' I called Decker and demanded to check on you. I told him that I'd drop the case if he didn't let me."

"He must have loved that," Jessie said because she didn't trust herself to say much more.

"Yeah, he threatened to fire me and hung up. But then he called back five minutes later and said he'd patch me through to you if I called the main number and asked for Marshal Murphy. Who's that?"

"He's part of my security contingent," she explained. "I don't think I'm supposed to even say that, actually."

"Right. Need to know, I get it. So how are you—really?"

Jessie was fine up until that last word. *Really.* Suddenly a floodgate of emotion opened and she felt a sob rising in her throat. At the last moment, she covered it with a cough.

"I've been better," she said, her voice on the verge of cracking but managing to hold steady. "It's hard dealing with all this without much of a support system around. After the escape from NRD, Kat is off finding herself in Europe. I haven't been able to see my therapist for security reasons. I haven't been allowed to talk to you. And until today, I've been essentially locked up in a safe house. The marshals are good at their job. But they're not exactly chatty Cathys. And I haven't been sleeping great, mostly because I'm in constant fear that one of two serial killers is going to find me."

"That sounds like a super fun time," Ryan replied with mock enthusiasm before returning to his normal voice. "I'm really sorry, Jessie. That sounds hellish."

"Thanks," she said.

There was a long pause that was just starting to get awkward when she broke the silence.

"How are you doing?" she asked, keeping things general though she was particularly curious about the state of his marriage. He had recently mentioned that he and his wife had separated.

"My life has been...topsy-turvy. I'll tell you more about when we can talk in person. Besides, it feels weird to complain about anything going on with me when you're under such duress."

"At least it's not boring," Jessie said, letting him off the hook for now.

"Yeah. Hopefully, both these guys will be caught soon and you can resume your normal life of not going out at night, watching boring television, and eating poorly."

"I would love that," she said, chuckling.

There was a soft knock on the door. Jessie knew what that meant.

"Hey. I'm being told to wrap it up. But don't be such a stranger, okay. I don't want you to lose your job or anything, but it's nice to hear from you every now and then."

"I'll see what I can do, as long as it doesn't put my pension at risk," he added jokingly. "You're not worth that."

"Nice," she said, hanging up before he could get sincere again.

She opened the door and gave the phone back to Murph.

"Let's get you somewhere out of the way," he said, not commenting on anything he may or may not have heard.

They returned to the conference room, which was now empty. Jessie grabbed a handful of potato chips and looked through her list of Claire's other dates from the LOL website.

There were two she was particularly interested in. One was the movie star. The other was a tech CEO. Both had dated her in the last three months, making their breakups more recent, and potentially, more raw.

She decided to call the actor's number first, working off the premise that securing an interview with him might prove more challenging than a CEO.

Jett Collison was a legitimate movie star. According to his Wikipedia page, he was only twenty-six. But he'd already headlined multiple blockbuster films. His specialty was playing the slightly nerdy, endearingly awkward but unconventionally good-looking and charming lead in romantic comedies. He was like a younger, American Hugh Grant type. Her adoptive mom, Janice, had loved

62

those 1990s Hugh Grant movies, watching them on repeat. Jessie thought that, were she still alive, she'd probably like Collison too.

Jessie called the number listed on his account and got a perky female voice.

"Jett's phone. This is Matilda. How can I help?"

"Hi, Matilda. I'm with the LAPD. Is Jett available?"

"Is this some kind of prank?" Matilda asked. "Is this Marnie? I know it's you."

"This isn't Marnie," Jessie said, snapping into her most professional tone. "My name is Hunt. I work with the LAPD. We're investigating a blackmail ring and we're concerned Mr. Collison might be a potential victim. We'd like to speak to him ASAP. Can you put him on, please?"

She waited for Matilda to demand more proof that Jessie was who she said she was. Instead she caved immediately.

"I'm sorry," Matilda said, sounding chastened. "But Jett is on set. The call sheet has him shooting almost non-stop until about eleven p.m. tonight. If I pull him, it could cost hundreds of thousands of dollars and maybe my job. Is there any way you could talk to him tomorrow? He's off all day."

Jessie was about to tear into Matilda when she looked at the clock. It was after 5 p.m. already and she still had to reach out to the tech CEO and see what Dolan had found on the Jerebko alibis. It was unlikely she could get to Collison today anyway. She decided to play nice.

"Here's what I need you to do, Matilda," she said, still firm but with less of an edge. "Go find your boss and speak to him privately. Tell him that LAPD is concerned that he might be at risk for blackmail related to a group called LOL. When he hears that, he'll know what it's about. Have him text me at this number with a location to discuss the matter first thing tomorrow. It's five-oh-seven p.m. now. If I don't get that text by seven p.m., my partner and I are going to come to that set and bring him into the station to chat, no matter what he's shooting. We clear?"

"Yes, ma'am," Matilda said.

"Have a nice evening," Jessie said before hanging up.

"You seemed to enjoy that more than was professionally appropriate," Murph said without looking up.

"What—are you the peanut gallery now?" Jessie asked, half-irked, half-amused. "You barely speak for hours at a time and then you bust out random critiques of my investigative techniques?"

"Just an observation."

Before she could reply the door opened and Dolan stepped in. He looked frustrated.

"What's the problem?" she asked.

"Jerebko's latest girlfriend confirmed his alibi," he said disappointed. "And his phone GPS data does too. We're checking video cameras from her building but it doesn't look good."

"What about Gayle?"

"Same. I didn't talk to her kids. But her phone data has her exactly where she said she was—at home. Your tech folks even found that she bought a movie on Amazon around eleven forty-five p.m. That doesn't totally absolve her. The medical examiner is putting time of death as between midnight and two a.m. But nothing I've found suggests she's an avenging angel. Besides, she struck me as a practical sort. She knows that a scandal like this isn't going to ruin her husband's reputation. Hell, it might even make him more interesting to voters. Either way, I think we've hit a dead end with the Jerebkos."

"That sucks."

"Yep. So I cut Milton loose, at least for now. And it gets worse. The preliminary toxicology report came back negative for drugs. Nothing official, but it looks like Claire had a little alcohol in her system. That was it."

"How is that worse?" Jessie asked.

"Because now the marshal over there is going to start thinking he should apply to the FBI."

"I'm happy with my gig," Murph said quietly, somehow managing not to smile.

"What a saint you are," Dolan said, looking more bothered by Murph being correct about Claire not being an addict than their top suspects alibiing out.

"Maybe I can improve your mood," Jessie said as she stood up, hoping to move on from the testosterone battle she felt brewing.

"How's that?" he asked, reluctantly turning his attention to her as she collected her things and started toward the conference room door.

"I have two more suspects for us to check out. One of them is a major tech CEO. I think we could surprise him in his office if we head out now."

"Sounds promising," Dolan said. "Who's the other one?"

"We'll have to hold off until tomorrow on that one. And I don't want you to get too giddy. But he's a real-life movie star. Bring your autograph book, Dolan."

She saw him open his mouth to offer a quippy retort. But before he could, she was out of the room, leaving him to talk to the door.

CHAPTER ELEVEN

They barely made it.

Even using the sirens, the drive from Central Station to Gunther Stroud's downtown high-rise office, less than ten miles away, took almost twenty minutes in LA's rush hour traffic.

Jessie had assumed that a big-time executive would work well past the time arrived—5:36. But when the elevator door opened to the thirty-seventh floor, Stroud was standing there, briefcase in hand, ready to leave. Behind him, the place looked quiet, other than a lone receptionist at the main desk.

He was in his late thirties, medium height, with glasses, tight, curly brown hair, and pale skin that suggested he didn't leave his office a lot. He seemed distracted and didn't even notice there were four people standing in front of him until Dolan spoke.

"FBI, LAPD, and Marshals Service, Mr. Stroud," he said, making the CEO jump slightly. "Mind if we take a moment of your time?"

The man's eyes opened wide for the briefest of seconds before he regrouped.

"What's this about?' he asked.

Jessie heard a hint of an accent, though she couldn't quite place it—maybe South African? Wherever he was originally from, Stroud had clearly been here for a long time.

"It's of a sensitive nature," Jessie said. "Why don't we go to your office?"

"I'm about to leave for the day," Stroud protested. "Tell me now."

Jessie knew that reaction wasn't going to go over well with Dolan and she was right.

"Okay, Mr. Stroud," he began, his voice carrying a bite it lacked before. "This is about a club you're a member of that pairs older, wealthy, sex-hungry men with younger women who wouldn't normally give them the time of day."

Stroud glanced back involuntarily at the receptionist before turning around.

"Let's go to my office," he hissed under his breath.

As they followed him, Dolan cracked the widest smile Jessie had ever seen from him. Jessie appreciated the dig but wondered how productive it was for getting the answers they needed. Now Stroud would be on the defensive for the rest of their interview.

As they approached his office, Toomey took up a spot just outside the office. Once the door closed, Murph did the same thing inside the office. Stroud turned to them and started talking before any of them could pose more questions.

"I am very busy. It's hard to find time to meet women. So I signed up for this website. It's not illegal. It's just a way to introduce people to each other. I didn't pay my dates for sex. I didn't promise anything. I don't know what I did wrong."

"Are you married, Mr. Stroud?" Jessie asked, already well aware of the answer.

He seemed taken aback, but only briefly.

"My wife is assigned to our London office. We don't get to see each other often. So we have an understanding. She knows I...go out."

"I wonder who "assigned' her to the London office?" Dolan cracked, enjoying amplifying his "bull in a china shop" persona.

"It was a mutual decision," Stroud said in a clipped tone.

"Do you know a woman named Claire Stanton?" Jessie asked, trying to get things back on track.

He didn't make any effort to hide his familiarity as his face broke into a pleasant smile at the thought of her.

"Yes, of course. Claire and I dated for several months a while back. She's a great girl."

"Why did you break up?" Jessie asked.

"She said she had met someone she felt strongly about and didn't feel right about continuing to see me."

"Did she give a name?"

"No," Stroud scoffed. "That wasn't her way. She was very discreet."

"So you believed her about meeting someone else?" Dolan asked, a little surprised.

"I didn't care. Whether she met someone or was lying, she clearly didn't want to see me anymore. So I accepted it and moved on. There are many pretty girls in Los Angeles."

"Where were you last night?" Jessie asked quickly, hoping the random barrage of questions might knock him off guard.

He looked perplexed for a moment before responding confidently.

"I was here."

"In the office?" she asked.

"Yes, we had a programming bug with our latest update and it was all hands on deck to resolve it. I was up all night working with the tech team."

"You didn't leave at any point during the night?" Dolan pressed.

"No. I crashed for a few hours on my couch around four a.m. but I was here the whole time. That's why I was anxious to leave just now—to go home and sleep."

"Who can verify your whereabouts last night?" Dolan asked.

Stroud looked at him like he was joking.

"Only about ten software engineers, our marketing and PR leads, our general counsel, and my personal assistant. There was a pizza guy here at one point too."

Jessie thought she could almost hear the energy leave the room.

"We'll need all their names," she said, though she doubted they would. "And we'll be checking with building security so we can review the security camera footage from last night."

"No problem," Stroud said, sensing the pressure on him easing. "My assistant keeps detailed logs. What is this all about anyway?"

"Thank you for your time, Mr. Stroud," Jessie replied, ignoring his question and handing over a card for Central Station's detective bureau. "Please have your assistant send those logs to this contact number. And don't leave town without contacting us first."

She left without another word. There was no reason to inform him of Claire's death unless it served their purposes. And for now, at least, it didn't.

As they took the elevator back down, no one spoke for several seconds.

"Well," Murph finally muttered, "that was deeply unsatisfying."

Jessie and Dolan both stared daggers at him. Before either could respond, her phone pinged and she looked down.

"How about that?" she said, brightening slightly. "It's a message from Matilda, Jett Collison's assistant. He would be happy to meet with us at his Malibu beach house tomorrow at nine a.m. The address is included."

"Why don't we just go over there now and interrogate him?"

Jessie looked at Dolan in stunned silence. It was Murph who finally replied.

"Do you really live in this town?" he asked incredulously. "What do you think is going to happen if an FBI agent, an LAPD criminal profiler, and two US Marshals show up on a film set and demand to question a famous actor? Do you think that's going to stay quiet for long? Do you think Hunt's protective status will be enhanced by that, with all the cell phone photos sent to TMZ within minutes of us arriving?"

"Is he really that big a deal?" Dolan asked, surprised by Murph's unusually strong response.

"He's a big deal," Murph assured him. "And if we show up and start throwing our weight around on a film set, we'll become a big deal pretty fast too. And that's generally not a good idea when we're trying to keep a low profile. Maybe we just go to his beach house tomorrow in our unmarked car and talk to him without an entire movie crew around. What do you think, Agent Dolan?"

Jessie had never seen Murph so incensed. Clearly Dolan hadn't either.

"Fine," he said, sounding a little pouty. "It's almost six anyway and I don't know what else we can do tonight. I say we knock off for the day. I could use a drink."

"We can drop you off somewhere," Murph said, "but we need to get Hunt back to the safe house. The night unit is taking over soon."

"You guys can join me for one drink," Dolan cajoled. "Come on, you can fill me in on how the movie industry really works."

"I'm up for a drink," Jessie said. Anything that kept her out of that carpeted residential prison was appealing to her, even if it meant having a drink with a pain like Dolan.

"Not happening," Murph said matter-of-factly.

"Come on," Dolan said. "Do you really think she'll be in danger in a randomly selected bar? In the last hour we've weaved in and out of rush hour traffic with a second car behind us for security. If we were being followed, you guys would know. You can even pick the bar, Marshal Murphy. That way you know neither Crutchfield nor

Thurman could anticipate our next location. What do you say, Murphy? Don't be a killjoy."

Jessie didn't join in the pile-on, certain that it was a waste of time. Instead she settled back in her seat, determined to enjoy what was left of her remaining free time tonight, even if it was only in a moving vehicle. She closed her eyes and tried to do a mini-meditation, focusing on her breath as her chest rose and fell slowly.

Her attention was diverted by the sound of Murph's voice on his comm.

"All teams. There will be a momentary delay in returning to home base. Unscheduled stop upcoming. Timing indeterminate. Details to follow. Follow car—stay frosty."

Jessie opened her eyes, unsure if she'd heard right.

Am I really going to a bar?

CHAPTER TWELVE

She was. But not right away. First, Murph hopped out to check out the place, called Bob's Frolic Four, while Toomey circled the block with Jessie and Dolan in the back. The bar was in a weird part of downtown. It was on a busy commercial street, but only two blocks west, the business district ended abruptly and they were in a residential area.

Suddenly the streets had speed bumps and "children at play" signs. The neighborhood, at the edge of the West Adams district, was comprised of an eclectic mix of cottage-style homes and grandiose mansions that looked to have been built before World War II.

But before Jessie could really appreciate them, Toomey had looped around and was headed back to the busy section lined with stores, restaurants, and bars. As they pulled around to the front of Bob's again, Toomey spoke to them. Hearing his voice was such a rarity that she almost forgotten how it sounded.

"Get out the second I stop," he instructed. "Murph is waiting at the door. Proceed directly inside. Follow all instructions without hesitation. Understood?"

"Understood," Jessie said.

"This just might be the best night of my life," Dolan added giddily as he nodded his assent.

The car stopped and they got out, moving briskly to the door, which Murph was holding open. He directed them through the crowded space to a back room, away from the other patrons.

When they got there, Jessie realized why Murph had been willing to accede to the request. This was a cop bar and the back room was almost exclusively law enforcement. She recognized a few detectives from nearby precincts as well as a few off-duty uniformed officers. There were others whom she didn't personally recognize but could peg as law enforcement based on their general bearing. Of the dozen people in the room, she guessed all but one were cops of some kind. And that one was the bartender.

Murph directed them to two unoccupied stools at the end of the small bar top. As they settled in, she heard him speak into his comm.

"Jabberjay and Pigeon are in place. Toomey, let me know when you are established in the front room. Collica, maintain position in the front of the location for now and do periodic checks around back. Emerson, continue to surveil the block from the vehicle. Anything unusual—let me know immediately."

When he was done, Dolan leaned over to him.

"Is my code name Pigeon?" he asked playfully. "That's kind of insulting, don't you think? A pigeon is just a rat with wings."

Murph just shrugged, as his eyes darted around the room, always moving.

"Don't complain," Jessie said. "It's better than Jabberjay. They're picking literary references to insult me."

"At least they got creative with you," Dolan said, before adding, "What literature are they referencing anyway?"

Jessie looked at him, amazed at his cluelessness.

"You are a pop culture black hole, Dolan," she said.

"And both of you are wasting time,' Murph noted quietly. "I'm giving you a half hour in here, tops. So you better order those drinks you were so excited about. And Jabberjay, cash only for you, got it? No credit cards. No names. Even here."

She nodded and waved down the bartender.

"Glenlivet—neat, please," she said then turned to Dolan. "What are you having, Pigeon?"

"Thanks," he said before turning to the bartender. "I'll have a glass of your cheapest bourbon, barkeep—a double please."

While they waited, Jessie got a text message from Captain Decker. After looking at it, she showed it to Dolan. It read: *Still no leads on BC or XT. Hospitals have nothing. CSI still checking Cortez's body but so far nothing. Stay positive. We'll get them.*

"Maybe you should make it a double too," Dolan said after reading it.

"Don't tempt me," she said as their drinks arrived.

She took a long slow sip, letting the sweet, warm burn of the liquid coat her throat. After swallowing, she turned back to her temporary partner.

"So now that it's just you and me in a bar, how about telling me the real reason you changed your mind this morning and backed the idea of me following up on the Stanton case?"

"What do you mean?" he asked before downing his shot and motioning for another.

She gave him her best "you've got to be kidding me" look.

"I mean, one minute you were ready to bail because the case had no connection to either Crutchfield or Thurman. It looked like I was headed back to that godforsaken safe house. And then you do a total one eighty and back me continuing to investigate, with your help. What gives?"

"I thought you deserved a chance," he said unconvincingly.

She just stared at him.

"Fine," he said eventually. "I'll give you the real reason. But it's gonna piss you off."

"So what's new? Spill."

"I figured the more you were out and about, pursuing the case, the more likely we were to stumble upon one of those guys. That couldn't happen if you were in the safe house locked away."

"So basically, you wanted to use me as bait to draw out two serial killers," she said.

"I wouldn't put it that way," he said, before downing the second bourbon that had just been placed before him. "Okay, I guess I would put it that way."

"And that's why you wanted to go to the film set tonight? You were hoping someone would shoot footage to tip off either Crutchfield or my father?"

"That wasn't my specific intent. But when I heard it could happen, I wasn't devastated," he admitted before turning and looking her straight in the eye. "Look, I don't believe we're going to catch these guys through standard shoe leather investigation. We have to draw them out, get them excited; hope they make a mistake. And the best way to do that is to make them come out of hiding and go after you. That's when they're most vulnerable."

His third drink arrived and he tossed it back while Jessie took another sip of hers.

"I guess I appreciate your honesty," she said. She had suspected this might be his reason but she hadn't expected him to come clean about it. He deserved credit for that at least.

"I'm a lot of things, but a liar isn't one of them," he said, before amending it a moment later. "Actually, that's not true. I am a liar; just not a congenital one. It's situation-specific."

"Man, you are one surly son of a bitch," she marveled. "How did you get that way?"

He looked over at her and raised his eyebrow. She thought she'd somehow offended him and decided to let the matter drop. But then he answered.

"Four years ago, my wife and son were killed in a hit and run by a bank robber," he said without emotion. "The guy was trying to escape and T-boned them. He walked away without a scratch. I've been in a bad mood ever since."

Jessie, in shock, coughed on her drink. It took her a good twenty seconds to recover.

"Jeez," she finally managed to croak, "I didn't know. I'm so sorry."

"Believe me, if there's anyone who doesn't have to show deference to me in the family tragedy department, it's you. Mother murdered by your serial killer father at age six. Left for dead in a freezing cabin with her body. Your husband turns out to be a sociopath who frames you for murder and then tries to kill you when you figure it out. Your long-lost father finds and butchers your adoptive parents. I'm surprised *you're* not more surly."

"Yeah, me too," Jessie agreed quietly.

Suddenly she didn't feel like drinking the rest of her scotch. Images of her adoptive parents, Bruce and Janine Hunt, flashed through her head. She tried not to think of the last ones; of them both dead in their senior living apartment. She tried to picture them when they were younger, teaching her to bake chocolate chip cookies and to ski on the bunny slopes of New Mexico. But the other, harsher, images kept intruding.

"I need to go to the restroom," she muttered, getting up from the stool.

Murph moved to follow her but she held up her hand.

"Can I please just get a single, solitary moment of privacy?" she asked tersely. "I'm not going anywhere. Just chat up your buddy there. I'll be back in a minute."

Murph stopped, though he didn't look happy about it. Jessie didn't care. She needed a few minutes alone to collect herself and it looked like the ladies' room of a cop bar was the only place she'd be able to get it.

She walked to the very back of the bar and pushed open the door to the ladies' room. Mercifully, it was empty. Even though she

74

didn't need to use the bathroom, she went to a stall and sat down, allowing herself a few seconds to let the ache of her most recent loss rise up in a few brief hiccupping sobs and then, ever so slightly, dissipate.

She would have liked to have stayed in there longer, alone with her thoughts. But she heard someone else come in and get in the other stall. The last thing she needed was a stranger hearing her cry. So she got out and went to over to the sink to wash her hands and throw a little water on her face.

She looked at herself in the mirror. The day had taken its toll. She was already sleep-deprived and stressed. But the mental exhaustion of the investigation seemed to make her skin sag more than usual. Only her green eyes, which had been so dull of late, actually looked better. Maybe it was the thrill of being on a case. Perhaps it was the dampness from her brief cry. But they sparkled with an energy that hadn't been there in recent days.

She heard the flush of the other stall and dabbed at the edges of her eyes quickly so whoever came out wouldn't notice. It was an ungainly woman in an ugly pantsuit with an unflattering perm. She looked like she'd already downed a few too many. A bit wobbly as she made her way to the sinks, the woman reached out to the counter to steady herself.

"You okay?" Jessie asked, glad the woman wasn't in any condition to notice somebody else's personal issues.

"Yes, thanks," the woman said wearily. "Long day. I may have overdone the whole 'taking the edge off' thing."

Jessie chuckled slightly.

"Believe me, I understand," she said as she leaned back in toward the mirror, making sure the tears from earlier hadn't left any smears from her minimal makeup.

"Thanks for not judging," the other woman said, glancing over and giving a half-smile as she touched up her hair in the mirror. "We all have burdens to carry that others can't comprehend, am I right?"

Jessie nodded in agreement. She was just tossing her paper towel in the trash slot on the counter when a tingling sensation ran down her spine. Something about the woman's half-smile caused a delayed flash of recognition, like an intense sense of déjà vu. It was familiar.

It was only as the woman reached into her purse that Jessie was able to place where she knew the smile from. It was a smile she'd seen so many times through the glass of a cell at the NRD prison facility. It was Bolton Crutchfield's smile.

CHAPTER THIRTEEN

Jessie didn't have time to react.

Before she could move or even speak, Crutchfield had slammed her into the wall and whipped a small knife out of the purse. He held it to her carotid artery, pressing the tip firmly against her skin. They were both facing forward, staring at each other in the bathroom mirror.

"Am I your beast of burden, Miss Jessie?" he purred in her ear in his agonizingly familiar Louisiana drawl.

In the middle of her heart-thumping panic, Jessie chastised herself for not realizing it was him earlier. The perm was clearly a bad wig. The pantsuit looked like something he'd found at a thrift shop specializing in 1980s women's wear. And up close, the hair on his arms was obvious, even if he had shaved and put pancake makeup and mascara on his face.

She'd been so polite, not wanting to judge this seemingly drunk, fashioned-challenged relic from another era that she'd missed the obvious warning signs. As she stared back silently at Crutchfield, she allowed her frustration with herself to rise up as her central emotion. It was preferable to fear.

He stared at her impassively, watching her, waiting to see how she'd react. She knew that what she said and did next might determine if she lived or died.

This was the first time she'd interacted with Crutchfield without him being locked up. Though the physical situation between them had changed, she decided their dynamic couldn't. She tried to quiet her mind, control the terror creeping out of her insides and remind herself why Crutchfield had helped her with cases in the past, why he enjoyed her visits, why he'd even warned her that her father was after her: he liked her.

And why does he like me?

Because I don't back down from him. Because I don't act like the helpless victim. Because I give as good as I get. Because, despite everything I've suffered, I'm a badass.

77

In that moment, she knew what to do. Despite the knife digging at her throat, Jessie felt her body relax. She stopped pressing against Crutchfield, stopped trying to break free, and allowed him to squeeze her tighter. She took a long, slow, languorous breath and exhaled deeply.

"Don't sell yourself short, Mr. Crutchfield," she said in a steadier voice than she imagined possible. "I wouldn't call you a beast, though you're hardly a prince either."

Crutchfield grinned despite himself, loosening his grip on her ever so slightly.

"Still a firecracker, even under these circumstances," he said appreciatively. "I've missed your company, Miss Jessie. You never cease to surprise."

Jessie took another breath, fairly certain now that he was unlikely to gut her like he had Ernie Cortez, at least not in the next few seconds.

"Nor you, Mr. Crutchfield," she replied smoothly. "I didn't know your taste in fashion was so retro. Are you going to a 'Working Girl' costume party later?"

Crutchfield broke out into a full smile at that reference.

"Oh, do I give off a Melanie Griffith sensibility?"

"More like Joan Cusack," she observed.

"Close enough," he said, pretending to be miffed. "While chatting old movies with you is delightful, we're low on time so I'll have to cut it short. I'll bet your marshal friend outside is getting a little nervous and debating how long is too long before busting into the ladies' room."

"Impertinent, he is," Jessie agreed, trying to keep the gabby vibe going so he didn't suddenly decide to get stabby.

"I hope we see each other again, Miss Jessie," he said, his voice turning serious. "But for that to happen, you have to survive the night. And in order to wake up tomorrow, you'll need to follow my advice. Don't go home tonight. Sometimes a safe house isn't as safe as it seems."

Jessie's eyes widened despite herself.

"Wait, are you saying my father is—"

"I hate to do this, Miss Jessie," he said, cutting her off. "But for us to reunite, I have to take my leave now. And to do that without interference, I need you…indisposed."

78

Before she could ask what that meant, Crutchfield's palm was on the back of her skull, slamming her forehead toward the mirror. The last thing she saw was her own face coming at her way too fast. Then there was a flash of agony, followed by blackness.

*

When she came to, she found herself slumped on the bathroom floor. Murph was standing over her, his gun drawn. She could hear his voice but couldn't quite make out the words. After a few seconds they unjumbled and she understood him.

"...me, Hunt. Are you all right? Can you hear me?"

"Uh-huh," she managed to groan.

A second later Dolan was in the bathroom too. He took one look at the situation and pulled out his sidearm as well. Murph glanced back at him briefly.

"Check on her," he ordered. "I need to secure the room."

If he hadn't yet secured the room, then that meant that he'd only just come in. She wondered how long she'd been out. Dolan knelt down beside her and studied her head. She knew she was bleeding because she could feel the liquid dribbling down her check, narrowly missing her right eye.

She kept her focus on Murph, who kicked in both stalls, then turned his attention to the small, open window along the far wall. He approached it from the side and carefully peeked out before quickly retreating and speaking into his comm.

"Day team—be advised. An assailant is in the area and was inside the location. Likely escaped through a restroom window. Suspect might still be in the alley or adjacent street. Toomey and Collica, circle the location from opposite directions and meet in back. Emerson—continue to drive around the block and await further instructions. High alert."

"Woman..." Jessie muttered.

"What?" Dolan asked, leaning in close.

"Crutchfield...dressed as a woman."

Dolan looked up at Murph.

"Hunt says it was Crutchfield and that he's dressed as a woman, or at least he was."

Murph nodded and returned to his comm.

"Be advised, suspect is B.C. He may be disguised as a woman. I need thirty-second check-ins from the ground team members," he said, then turned back to Jessie and Dolan. "How's she doing?"

"Yeah, how *is* she doing?" Jessie repeated.

"Little cut above the right temple," Dolan said. "Probably doesn't even need stitches. A small bandage should do it. He could have done far worse."

"He wasn't really trying to hurt me. He wanted to warn me."

"About what?" Dolan asked.

"The safe house. He said it wasn't safe."

Murph looked crestfallen for a moment before his attention returned to the voice in his ear. After listening, he looked even more deflated.

"All teams have checked in," he told them. "They didn't find anything. He's gone."

CHAPTER FOURTEEN

They decided Jessie should stay at the station for the night.

She would have protested but under the circumstances, it was out of her hands. Besides, she didn't have any better ideas. Of course, when they said "station," she didn't realize they meant a cot in an unoccupied cell.

"Am I being punished?" she asked Captain Decker.

"No," he told her as they all walked down the deserted hall to the lockup area. "This is actually the safest possible place for you, at least in the short term. This holding cell is isolated from the others so we can keep your presence a secret from most folks. It's secure and monitored 24/7. For tonight, the security team includes two of my most trusted officers. Dolan is going to sleep in the other cot in the room. And four fresh US marshals will be here in twenty minutes to relieve Murphy's team for the night. You can't do much better than this, unless you're in a fallout bunker."

"So, not punishment then," she said, more to lighten the mood than to be combative. Before he could come back at her she turned to Murph. "Is everyone at the safe house okay?"

"All good so far," he said. "We've increased the tactical team contingent in the hopes that your father shows up but they're mostly off-site. We're using additional surveillance, including drones. We want to draw him in, actually. We've even got a female marshal walking around in your clothes with her hair done up in a ponytail like yours. She's armed to the teeth, so even if he gets in, he's in for a surprise."

"Don't get cocky, Murph," Jessie advised. "Xander Thurman is devious, patient, and brilliant. Underestimating him usually gets people killed."

"We've got it covered, Ms. Hunt," he assured her firmly.

"Whatever you say," she said, then turned her attention back to Decker. "By the way, am I allowed any more ibuprofen or is that against jail rules? My head is still killing me."

"The doctor said you could have two more at eleven p.m. but not before."

"And she really didn't think I had a concussion?" Jessie recalled incredulously. "You buying that?"

"You heard the same thing as me," Decker replied. "She thinks the blow was hard enough to daze you but not enough to concuss you; almost like he'd perfected the technique."

"Crutchfield has perfected a lot of techniques," Jessie agreed, "including apparently finding me in that bar somehow. Any theories on how that happened?"

Murph stepped forward and spoke. He sounded almost mechanical.

"We think he set up a stakeout location in the area around Central Station, knowing you'd show up at some point. Our guys did a search of buildings around the station and found a whole setup in an unoccupied apartment across from the station's garage entrance. There was an empty pizza box and several empty soda bottles. His prints were on them. We think he waited and watched from there all day long. He likely noticed our vehicle coming and going throughout the day. It's not the same make and model as typical unmarked LAPD vehicles, which was a sloppy mistake on our part. We suspect he saw us leave and followed us to the bar."

"Any plan to remedy that in the future?" she asked, trying not to sound too accusatory.

"We've got your officers canvassing the area in shifts. And, on the off chance that he's set up another stakeout that we don't find, we plan to use unmarked police vehicles for any future trips so he can't distinguish among them."

"That might solve one problem," Dolan noted. "But it doesn't explain how he disappeared from a bar on a busy city block without a trace."

"That alley didn't have any cameras," Decker noted. "But both the adjoining streets did. Our team didn't see anyone leave the area in the outfit you described or who looked like Crutchfield usually does."

"It's possible he had other clothes waiting in the alley," Jessie said, "or something else under that pantsuit. Or he could have…"

She trailed off, hesitant to suggest her other theory.

"What?" Decker asked.

"Knowing him, he may have gotten creative—maybe pulled up a manhole cover and escaped through the sewer. I doubt that kind of thing would bother him."

"We didn't check the sewers," Decker admitted.

"He would have had to be pretty fast before my guys got there," Murph said. "Even if he planned that ahead of time, it would be tight."

"We don't know how long he had," Jessie reminded him. "I could have been out for seconds or minutes."

"It was seconds," Murph said confidently.

"How can you be sure?"

"Because the fog from your breath where he held you against the mirror hadn't faded when I came in. By the time Dolan arrived, less than fifteen seconds later, it was gone. So from the time he hit your head against the mirror until I burst in was less than that. I probably missed him by the blink of an eye. He would have had less than thirty seconds to get from the window to the closest manhole cover, open it, get in, and close it before Toomey or Collica got there. That's tight."

"But probably exactly what happened," Dolan said as kicked off his shoes, lay down on a cot, and stretched out. "Someone should check down there to see if he ditched his clothes. Maybe there's evidence on them that can help pinpoint where he's been hiding."

"Are you really going to just crash right now?" Jessie asked, amazed.

"Nope," he replied. "First I'm going to wrap this scratchy blanket around myself. Then I'm going to crash."

Jessie turned back to the others, who were equally stunned. Murph recovered first.

"It's not a bad idea," he said. "You should get settled in. Someone will bring you that ibuprofen. But the sooner you can get to sleep, the more effective you'll be tomorrow. Assuming you still want to go out tomorrow."

Jessie gave him a dirty look. She was about to add a snarky reply when the sound of loud snoring from Dolan's cot echoed through the cell.

"Can someone get me earplugs too?" Jessie asked.

*

83

Jessie didn't get much sleep.

Part of it might have been Dolan's snoring. But she suspected she would have had problems even if he was silent. Her racing thoughts were more of an issue. Truthfully, having him in the cell, even with the noise, was more comforting than frustrating. Not that she would ever tell him.

Around 5 a.m. she gave up on sleep and got up to take a shower, change into the extra clothes the overnight marshals had brought from the safe house, and get some coffee. When she returned with a cup for him an hour later, he was curled up on the cot in the fetal position. His snoring had been replaced by a soft whistling wheeze.

She was tempted to let him sleep longer. But they needed to check the status of the Crutchfield and Thurman searches and see if the medical examiner had anything new on Claire Stanton. And all that was before making the trek to Malibu to meet with Jett Collison.

So, with more satisfaction than she was proud of, she gave Dolan's cot a hard kick. He snorted loudly and rolled over, barely catching himself before toppling over onto the floor.

"What the..?" he muttered.

"Rise and shine, Double Bourbon," Jessie said in her most intentionally annoying chipper tone.

Dolan's only response was to pull the blanket over his face and shoot her the middle finger.

"Oh, obscene finger gestures from such a demure FBI agent," she teased.

"I'm not that demure," he muttered from under the blanket.

"I got some coffee for you, Sunshine," she chirped happily. "Then we've got to get to work."

"Are you kidding?" he moaned. "Maybe in a couple of hours."

"In a couple of hours, we need to be halfway to Malibu to interview a movie star," she reminded him. "Before that, we've got overnight reports on Claire and our dual killers to review. Time is going to fly by."

"You don't want to sit this one out after what happened last night?" he asked.

"I realize we haven't known each other very long, Dolan. But I'm kind of shocked that you're even asking me that question. Are you still drunk?"

"Hey, I'm just looking out for you. You don't have to be so mean about it," he said, his head still hidden under the blanket. "Can I at least hit the head first?"

"You bet, Double Bourbon," she said. "I'll be waiting for you in the conference room."

By the time he joined her a half hour later with a muffin on one hand and a massive coffee in the other, she'd already read the ME report on Claire, which didn't have anything new. They also thought keys were the likely murder weapon. But her throat was so mangled that they couldn't make any determination about their style, make, or age. In addition, all the blood had flushed out the area around the skin, so there wasn't enough leftover bacteria to test for clues. They were back at square one on forensic evidence.

She tossed Dolan the file as he sat down and was about to open the overnight search reports on Crutchfield and Thurman when Decker walked in.

"I've got some updates," he said, his voice suggesting they ought not to get too excited.

"Good news, I gather," Dolan said sarcastically.

Decker launched in, ignoring the comment.

"Our CSU went back and checked the manhole and sewers near the bar. Sure enough, Crutchfield's prints were on the cover. We found the clothes Hunt referenced about ten yards down the tunnel, partially submerged in the sewer water. There was no way to get useful samples from them. We checked subsequent prints on every manhole cover for the next quarter mile and found one that led to an alley near a metro station. Camera footage shows him entering the station and then a bathroom. There was no footage of him leaving, but we sent a team there and found a maintenance worker unconscious in the bathroom storage closet. He was naked."

"Kinky," Dolan said, his mouth full.

"At least he wasn't killed," Jessie noted, relieved.

"That is good news," Decker agreed. "But that's about the only good news we have. When we checked the footage for a maintenance worker leaving the bathroom, we found one we think was Crutchfield. But he joined a group of others in an employee lounge. When our people arrived, they found the lounge had a back exit without working surveillance cameras. He got away."

"You think he deactivated the camera beforehand?" Jessie asked.

"No. It had been inoperable for a week before he escaped from NRD. He just got lucky."

There was a brief silence that was interrupted by Murph stepping into the room and tapping the lead overnight marshal on the shoulder. The other man left and Murph took his place without a word. His eyes were a bit puffy but otherwise, he looked fine.

Jessie was about to make a crack at his expense but Dolan spoke first.

"Any hits on Thurman?"

"Nothing," Decker answered. "He's been completely radio silent. I think his injuries may be keeping him out of commission more than we anticipated."

He was about to continue when the conference room phone rang. He picked up and listened, his face getting more ashen with each passing second. When he hung up, he looked straight at Jessie.

"I maybe have spoken too soon," he said, his voice thick with emotion.

"What do you mean?" she asked.

"A man matching Thurman's description attacked a detective earlier this morning, stabbing him multiple times."

"Who?" Dolan asked.

Jessie already knew the answer before Decker replied.

"Ryan Hernandez."

CHAPTER FIFTEEN

Jessie felt her heart drop into her stomach.

"He's alive," Decker continued before she could speak. "He's in surgery now. They're confident he's going to pull through."

"Did they catch Thurman?" Dolan asked immediately.

"No. The team was searching for evidence in a wooded area in Topanga Canyon. It was dark. Hernandez managed to fend him off after the first few cuts. He even fired off a shot. Good thing too because that's what alerted the rest of the team. By the time they arrived, he was barely conscious."

"Where was he stabbed?" Jessie asked with an even voice, betraying no hint that her concern was more than just professional.

"Once in the stomach just below the left ribs and several times in the left forearm. It sounds like he tried to block the blows with his arm."

"Did he think he hit Thurman when he fired?" Dolan wanted to know, seemingly oblivious to Hernandez's medical situation.

"Don't know at this point," Decker said. "If he did, it obviously wasn't a kill shot because they didn't find the guy. All Hernandez said before he passed out was that it looked like Thurman."

"How bad are the wounds?" Jessie asked, again noting that she sounded shockingly even-keeled.

"One forearm cut went down to the bone but they feel good about it in general. No major arteries were severed and they wrapped it tight. The abdomen wound is what concerns them. They're worried it might have gone deep enough to puncture a kidney. He apparently lost a fair bit of blood before they could get him to the hospital. The canyon was isolated and access was challenging. They used a helicopter."

The magnitude of the situation settled in among them and no one said anything for several seconds.

"Where is he?" Jessie finally asked. "I'm going to see him."

"No," Murph said firmly from the corner of the room.

"It's not a request," Jessie replied. "I've worked with Ryan Hernandez. He's not just a colleague. He's a friend. And he was attacked by *my* father because of *me*. I'm going to the hospital."

"No," Murph repeated, unmoved.

Jessie started for the door when Dolan put a hand gently on her arm.

"Hold up just a second before you go," he said in an unexpectedly soft voice. "Just think this through for a moment."

"Think what through?"

"Do you really believe that Hernandez managed to fend off your father? I know he's a good detective. But he was taken by surprise in the dark by an experienced killer. Does it sound like Hernandez is alive because of his skills or for some other reason?"

"What are you talking about?" Captain Decker asked, not following.

But Jessie did. Despite her anger and anxiety, the gears in her head began turning. Dolan was right. If Thurman had gotten close enough to stab Ryan in the abdomen, then he was close enough to have stabbed him in the chest or head or to have slit his throat. Ryan was alive because her father didn't intend to kill him.

But why would he let him live?

The second she asked herself the question, the answer was obvious. Dolan clearly knew it too as he was looking at her expectantly. She said out loud what they both realized.

"Thurman didn't kill Ryan because he wanted him to be taken to the hospital. He would have followed the helicopter from the ground to see where they took him. He knows I'd feel responsible for Detective Hernandez's injuries and want to see him. He couldn't find me any other way so he created a way. He's waiting for me at the hospital."

Dolan nodded in agreement.

"And that's why you absolutely can't go," he said.

"But *we* can," Decker noted emphatically. "We can flood the hospital with officers to look for him. This might actually be our chance to turn the tables on him."

"Or," Murph suggested from the corner, "you could go a less overt route and do what we did last night. Have someone who looks like Hunt go to Hernandez's room. Give him a wide berth. Then, if he shows up, pounce."

"That didn't work too well for you last night," Decker countered.

"Do you stop fishing and go home because your first piece of bait didn't work?" Murph asked. "Or do you put another piece of bait on the line, drop it in the water, and settle in for the long haul?"

Decker was apparently a fisherman because he nodded at the analogy.

"We'll set it up," he said before turning to Jessie. "You stay far away from that hospital. You're lucky I don't keep you locked in that cell until this is all over with."

"Captain, do you really think anywhere is secure for me until this is all over with? The best way to keep me safe is to catch the people who want to do me harm."

"Easy for you to say," Decker retorted gruffly. "If you die, the commissioner will execute me herself."

"How does Malibu sound for far away?" Dolan suggested, clearly sensing this dispute couldn't end well and quickly moving on. "I can't think of any better way to get your mind off this than to interrogate a real-life movie star. You in?"

"I'm in," Jessie said, following his lead.

Besides, as far as mental distractions went, this was a pretty good one.

*

As Toomey drove along Pacific Coast Highway and Santa Monica gave way to Malibu, they passed one beautiful home after another. But after forty-five minutes of oceanfront driving, they came to one that was different.

Jessie tried to hide her awe.

Despite her concern about Ryan, she couldn't help but be amazed at what she saw.

She'd been to some pretty stunning houses. She'd even lived in one for a while before learning her husband was sociopathic killer. But she'd never encountered anything like this.

Set apart from the other houses, which often only had just a few feet of space between them, this one was on an enclosed estate, resting on a cliff that dangled arrogantly over the water. It was the home of Jett Collison.

The three-story-tall Spanish-style mansion was surrounded by an elaborately designed twelve-foot stone wall that looked like it had been shipped in from Spain itself. The gate appeared to be made of thick wood but was actually metal delicately painted multiple hues of brown. In the distance, the Pacific Ocean stretched as far as the eye could see.

They parked in front of the gate. Even as Murph got out of the car, the perkily familiar voice of Jett Collison's assistant, Matilda, came over the intercom.

"Hi, are you with Hunt?" she asked. Jessie realized she'd never given the girl her first name. Apparently Matilda thought it was "Hunt." That was fine, as it made it less likely she'd be identified.

"Yes," Murph said, seemingly feeling the same way. "We're all part of her team."

"Could you please hold up your identification to the camera?" she asked politely.

Murph pulled it out and was about to unfold it to the photo page inside when the gate opened. Apparently Matilda was satisfied with seeing the exterior of a leather wallet.

Murph shrugged at Toomey as he returned to the passenger seat and got in.

"She's a sharp one," Toomey muttered under his breath.

They drove up the stone path to the main entrance of the house. As they arrived, Matilda came out to meet them. She didn't look like Jessie expected based on her voice. Short and heavyset, with glasses and a thick mop of curly dark hair, the only hint that this was the same person from the phone was the way she bounced on her toes, as if she couldn't control her own energy. She couldn't have been more than twenty-three years old.

"She looks more like an excitable librarian than an entertainment professional," Dolan said.

"How is an entertainment professional supposed to look, Agent Dolan?" Jessie asked sharply, taking her annoyance at her own assumptions out on him.

He looked at her, slightly taken aback, but said nothing. Jessie got out, trying to set aside her frustration with herself. Despite her training and experience, she still repeatedly made the cardinal sin of drawing conclusions before the evidence supported them. Just because Dolan had done the same thing didn't excuse her. She was supposed to be a criminal profiler, using facts to make assessments, not prejudging people based on how they looked or sounded.

I have to get better at this.

She plastered on a smile as she exited the car and walked over to shake hands.

"Hi, Matilda," she said in her warmest voice, "I'm Hunt."

"So nice to meet you," Matilda said, shaking her hand vigorously. "I'm sorry we couldn't make it work last night. But these darn studios, not wanting to waste millions of dollars an hour, right?"

"Sure," Jessie replied because she couldn't think of a snappier response.

"Hi, guys," Matilda said, waving as she took in the sight of the three other men as they got out of the car. "I didn't realize there would be so many of you. I only chilled one Perrier."

"That's okay," Dolan said drily. "I prefer tap water anyway."

"Still it is," Matilda said enthusiastically before turning to Murph and Toomey. "And for you gentlemen?"

Murph shook his head. Toomey didn't respond at all.

"They're good," Jessie said quickly. "Why don't we go inside? I think Mr. Toomey here is going to remain outside. He's a tad claustrophobic."

"It's a really big house, Mr. Toomey," Matilda promised. "Are you sure?"

Toomey gave a half nod. Matilda shrugged and beckoned for the others to follow her in the house as Toomey took up a position by the front door, facing back down the driveway.

"Jett only just got up," Matilda told them as she led them down a hallway with what appeared to be quartzite floor tiles underfoot. "He didn't wrap for the night until after midnight and he didn't get back here until after one. So he's still easing into the day."

"We'll try not to harsh his mellow too much," Dolan promised.

"I feel like you're teasing me a little," Matilda said playfully, though her smile seemed a bit forced.

"Just a little," Dolan replied as they rounded the corner and suddenly stepped into a massive room.

It was easily fifty yards long, with a thirty-foot-high vaulted ceiling. The entire length of the room was covered in floor to ceiling windows looking out on the Pacific. The side of the room closest to them looked like a cross between a retro bar and an arcade, with old-timey stand-up video games along the walls and the center area comprised of a ping-pong table, a billiards table, a foosball table, and an air hockey table. At the far end of the room was a huge, almost theater-sized screen against the back wall. Surrounding it in a loose semicircle were multiple couches and easy chairs.

"Jett," Matilda called out, her voice echoing loudly. "Your guests are here."

A head popped up from one of the couches and the arm attached to it waved them over. As they did, he got up to meet them.

Jett Collison looked much as he did in the movies that made him famous. He was tall, probably six foot two. Though he appeared lanky at first glance, Jessie saw that his biceps were bulging through his slightly-too-small T-shirt, which also exposed the bottom half of his well-defined abs.

His brown hair was uncombed and stuck up in places and he wore thin wire-rimmed glasses that highlighted his bright blue eyes. He gave them his patented lopsided grin as he loped over. He looked a bit like a slightly uncertain baby fawn wearing loose sweatpants. His bare feet made a slapping noise on the tiled floor.

As he came over, Jessie found herself almost unwittingly being charmed by his foppish, self-deprecating manner. She reminded herself that this guy made his living playing into that impression and not to be dazzled by it. After all, this could be the person who jammed multiple keys into Claire Stanton's throat less than thirty-six hours ago.

As he got closer, she could see that behind his winning smile and unconventional good looks, those blue eyes were full of apprehension. He knew this wasn't going to be a schmoozefest. She locked on to his concern, hoping to use it to her benefit.

"Guys," Matilda said by way of introduction, "this is Jett Collison. Jett, this is...oh jeez, I just realized I don't any of your names other than Hunt there."

"Jack Dolan," the FBI agent said as he shook Collison's hand, not identifying his agency.

"Murphy," Murph volunteered from several feet away, making no effort to shake hands.

"Nice to meet you all," Collison said, his voice soft and hesitant. "Sorry I'm so sloppy this morning. I'm not an early riser."

"Not a problem," Jessie said, smiling broadly in the hope that she could lull Collison into viewing her as more fan girl than interrogator. Maybe he'd be more forthcoming if he didn't view her as a serious threat. "Where should we talk?"

"Is the couch cool?" he asked uncertainly.

"Sure," she replied. "Lead the way, Mr. Collison."

"Okay. But only if you call me Jett," he said, as Jessie anticipated he would.

"Okay, Jett," she said, offering her biggest grin.

When they were all seated on various couches, Jett leaned back.

"So what's this all about?" he asked, trying to sound casual but failing.

"Well," she began, "we assume Matilda told you this was related to LOL, right?"

"Yes, ma'am," he said, looking like he was waiting for the hammer to drop.

"What can you tell us about your involvement in that organization?" she asked sweetly.

"Um, well, it's like a dating service, kind of. It helps guys meet up with girls to, you know, like, date and stuff."

Jessie wondered if his halting answers were due to nervousness or if he was just like this. If it was the latter, the writers of his movies deserved enormous credit.

"And you used this service?" she pressed.

"Yeah, I mean, sometimes. I met some cool girls through it. It's hard to meet girls in my regular life. So this is a little more... simple."

"You're not dating anyone seriously?" she asked.

"Well, that's a little complicated. Are we off the record here?"

"We're not reporters, Jett," Dolan said, adopting a dad tone. "We're law enforcement. Nothing is off the record."

"That said," Jessie jumped in, "if something you tell us isn't relevant to our investigation, we don't necessarily have to include it in our report."

"Um..." Jett hesitated.

Jessie could tell he needed a little push.

"Hey, Matilda," she said to the girl, who was standing just off to the side of the group rocking back and forth ever so slightly, "I think I'd love that Perrier now. And Jack would like his tap... er, still water too."

"Sure thing, Hunt," Matilda said, her voice friendlier than her expression. She left, though she clearly wanted to stick around. When she was out of earshot, Jessie resumed.

"Look, Jett. We obviously know you used the service or we wouldn't be here. And we know that the service pairs up wealthy men with young ladies who are open to all kinds of relationships, even really short-term ones. We're not here to bust you for soliciting prostitution, if that's what you're worried about. We just need information, okay?"

"Okay, cool," Jett said, running his fingers through his hair so that it jutted out even farther. "I just, okay, here's the thing. My publicist set me up with this actress, right? It helps get good press and I have someone to take to premieres and stuff. And she's cool and all. But we're not like, a real couple. It's more for show. But I still want to have some romance and stuff, you know. So a friend recommended this site and said it's all really discreet. I tried it out and liked it. I could go out with a girl...or usually stay home with her, and not worry that the paparazzi would be all over it."

"How could you be so sure?" Jessie asked.

"Well, I guess I couldn't be *totally* sure. But my friend said the company has never had a problem like that. Most of these girls don't work normal jobs. Their job is to date. The guys pay for all meals and clubs and sometimes a lot more, like rent and stuff. So if you're a girl who's looking to have fun, get wined and dined by some rich dude and not have to worry about paying your bills, it's a pretty good gig. Why would you risk messing it up by blabbing about it, you know?"

"You felt secure based on that alone?" Dolan followed up.

"Yeah, that and the fact that all my dates pretty much proved it was true. I never had one of these girls threaten me with some video or pump me for money, probably because I handed it out without being asked. I've paid for rent; for plane tickets for a girl to go home for Christmas. I once even bought a girl a puppy. I have the money. It made them happy. And the happier my date is, the better time we have. I'm not saying it's the most romantic thing in the world. But it works for everyone involved."

It was moments like this that made Jessie glad they'd been able to keep Claire's name out of the news. Officially it was so the next of kin could be notified. But the real reason was so that they could get genuine reactions about her from potential suspects.

With that in mind and without any warning, she asked the question she'd been setting him up for.

"Did it work for Claire Stanton?"

CHAPTER SIXTEEN

There was a long pause as Jett's eyes went wide.

When he started to answer, his voice cracked and he broke out in a dry cough that took several seconds to stop. Jessie couldn't tell if it was sincere or just a stalling technique.

He chugged some of the water on the coffee table and wiped his mouth.

"I think so," he finally said. "She seemed to be happy with the arrangement."

"How long did the two of you date?" Jessie asked.

"For a while, actually," he said. "It was more long term than some of the others. Once we started seeing each other, I kind of stopped dating the other girls."

"Why is that?" Dolan asked.

"Because I liked her," Jett said simply. "She was cool. I mean, she's super hot too, obviously. But she's also fun in a down to earth kind of way. We didn't always have to get bottle service in a club's VIP room. She was happy hanging out here, watching a movie and eating popcorn."

"But you stopped seeing her?" Jessie asked leadingly.

"Yeah. Filming got hectic. I couldn't really spend as much time with her as she wanted. She needed more financial security, you know? So we kind of parted ways, at least for now. Maybe we'll hook up again when the movie's done shooting. Is Claire in some kind of trouble? Has she done something wrong?"

"Nothing like that," Dolan assured him, apparently deciding to adopt Jessie's sugar over vinegar interrogation approach. "We're just doing some routine follow-up. Hey, can I ask you a few questions about your schedule the last few days?"

"Yeah, sure," Jett said. "But we might need to talk to Matilda if you want real details. She handles all that stuff."

"That's fine," Dolan said. "We'll start with you and she can help fill in the gaps, cool?"

"Cool," Jett agreed.

"Hey, Jett," Jessie interrupted, sensing this was the best moment to follow up on a suspicion she couldn't shake. "While Jack's asking you that stuff, can I use your restroom?"

"Sure, it's that way," he said, pointing to the hallway near the huge television screen.

She headed in that direction while Dolan continued his questioning. Murph made a move to follow her but she shook her head almost imperceptibly. He looked irked but stayed put.

Once she was out of sight, Jessie moved fast. Something about Jett's reaction to her question about how his relationship with Claire ended didn't ring genuine. And she suspected that she'd get more insight into the true nature of it by checking out where he lived rather than what he said. That meant finding his bedroom.

But how do I do that in a place this gigantic?

As she walked down the hall, she came to a carpeted stairwell that looked worn down, as if it dealt with lots of foot traffic. It was as decent a place to start as any. She jogged up the stairs two at a time, well aware that once Matilda returned with the waters, her absence would be noted.

Once on the second floor, she looked at the carpeting more closely and followed the section with the most shoe imprints. Sure enough, it led to a door at the end of a long hall. It was slightly ajar. Jessie briefly debated whether that met the legal standard for her to go in without being accused of breaking and entering.

After half a second, she decided to worry about that later and pushed the door open. It was clearly Jett's bedroom, as evidenced by the posters of his various movies, including, *The Bridegroom*, *Farmers Market*, and *The Bridegroom 2*.

The California king bed sat at one end of the huge room, with a view out the balcony doors to the beach and ocean. In the middle of the room was a treadmill, an elliptical machine, and a home gym. Against the other wall was a TV screen a mere third the size of the one in the living room.

She walked around, looking at the end table beside his bed, which had a script, a box of tissues, and a picture of an older couple she assumed were his parents. There was nothing else of personal note anywhere in the area. On the treadmill dashboard was a copy of *Entertainment Weekly*, open to a review of his latest movie, *Wing Man*. It got a B-minus.

97

She moved on to the bathroom. It was bigger than most bedrooms. She found more scripts and entertainment magazines strewn about, but nothing personal. The shower was standard, as was the steam room, other than the fact that he had a steam room.

She turned on the light in the walk-in closet and looked around. It was cavernous. But other than one section with suits and tuxes, almost everything in his wardrobe was casual. There were countless T-shirts and pairs of jeans.

She was just about to turn off the light and rush back down to the living room when she glanced at the far end of the closet, where Jett's coats rested on hangers. What drew her attention to them was that they were set apart from his other jackets.

Next to the suits and tuxes, he had a windbreaker, a leather jacket, a trench coat, and a ski parka. But at the far end were three heavy overcoats arranged in a line so as to block any view of the wall behind it.

Why does he have three overcoats when he lives in Southern California? Why are they all the way over there? He's got more than enough room to put them with his other coats over here.

She walked over to check it out. As she got closer, she immediately noticed something. There was a draft.

Jessie was wearing casual slacks and practical flats with ankle-high socks. Just above the top of the sock line, there was the hint of a breeze tickling the exposed skin. When she stopped walking and stood right in front of the overcoats, the cuffs of her pants billowed ever so slightly.

She pushed the coats to the side and looked at the wall behind them. It was immediately apparent that there was something behind it. Tiny rays of light snuck through a barely visible slit between sections of the wall. Jessie tapped on a section near the slit. It was hollow. She felt around until she found a notch the protruded out from the wall slightly and pressed on it. It gave way and the wall panel popped open, revealing a room behind it.

Jessie took a deep breath and stepped inside, looking around. The room seemed innocuous, almost as if it was a panic room without the security measures. There was a twin bed in one corner. Against the back wall was a chair with a small desk with a spiral notebook on it. She walked over and thumbed through it. It was comprised of handwritten short stories, general musings and poems—nothing horribly offensive. The room really did seem to be a temporary safe room in which to hole up if a crazed fan busted into the house.

Jessie sat down in the chair, disappointed. She realized she'd been harboring unreasonable hopes that the room would provide obvious evidence of Collison's guilt. It wouldn't have been the first time that a stalker kept hidden mementos of the target of his obsession. It fact, it was fairly common. But apparently Jett Collison was just a twenty-something actor who liked easy relationships with hot chicks and didn't want to get murdered by a psycho fan.

She put her elbows on her thighs and rested her head in her hands with her eyes closed, trying to determine where else to go with the case. Collison was their last serious suspect. If he didn't pan out, they'd be back to culling through old messages from the dating site and trying to make connections from dubiously relevant texts. The prospect wasn't appealing but it was all they had.

She opened her eyes again, determined to embrace the slog that was investigative work. Not every case got solved because of a brilliant flash of insight. In fact, far more often it was simple shoe leather investigating.

She was about to get up and go downstairs when she saw a small plastic bin underneath the twin bed across the room. She walked over and knelt down, tugging it out. There was something inside but the white bin's coating made it hard to see. The top was sealed shut like a Tupperware container but she managed to pry it open.

Inside was a small photo album. She opened it and gasped. Every picture was of Claire Stanton. A few were posed but most were candids. Some were obviously taken surreptitiously. A few were of her lying asleep in the bed in the bedroom, naked.

She put the album down and looked at the other two items in the box. One was another sealed container, this time smaller and circular. She popped it open. Inside was what amounted to a fistful of human hair. It was same shade of blonde as Claire's.

The last item was in a Ziploc bag. Jessie didn't open it as she could see inside it clearly. It held some kind of torn white cloth, maybe a ripped-off section of a scarf or kerchief. In one corner of the material was a red stain. It was hard to tell what it was—maybe lipstick, possibly blood.

She was leaning in to get a closer look when she heard a floorboard creak off to her right. Before she could react, a loud voice shouted at her.

"What the hell are you doing in here?"

CHAPTER SEVENTEEN

It was Matilda.

She stood at the entrance of the room, scowling and red-faced. Her whole body seemed to be vibrating with fury. Jessie glanced at her hands quickly and saw, to her relief, that they were empty.

"I was looking for a bathroom," Jessie said in what she hoped was a calming voice as she stood up, still ready for any sudden moves.

"In here?" Matilda demanded, still looking ready to pounce.

"I got turned around," Jessie explained. "Did you know about this room?"

"No. But maybe that's because I don't go snooping around my boss's house—because it's rude."

"Like I said," Jessie repeated with a consciously offhand demeanor, "I got a bit lost. It's a big house, Matilda, as you know."

"You need to get out of here!"

"You bet," Jessie agreed. "Let's head back down together so I don't get lost again."

"You can go on your own. I'm closing this up."

"I don't think so," Jessie said shortly.

"What?"

"We're going down together," Jessie announced, spreading her feet shoulder-length apart and flexing her fingers in anticipation of having to use them.

Matilda looked equally flummoxed and furious.

"You don't get to order me—"

"I'm afraid I do," Jessie cut her off. "I work with the Los Angeles Police Department and this room is potential evidence in a crime investigation. So I won't be leaving you alone in it. We are going downstairs together. That can happen with you walking in front of me, leading the way in a hospitable manner. Or I can cuff you and drag you back. Your call, Matilda."

For a second, the younger woman looked like she wanted to deck Jessie. But before she could react, someone behind her spoke.

"Everyone okay in here?" Murph asked, stepping into view. His tone was casual but Jessie could see that he was tense with anticipation.

"This woman is invading my boss's private space!" Matilda griped.

Murph nodded understandingly.

"She can be a bit intrusive," he said soothingly. "Why don't we all go downstairs and work it out together."

Matilda continued to stare angrily at Jessie. But after a few moments she seemed to regain her senses. She gave one last dirty look, then spun on her heel and muttered, "Follow me."

Once downstairs, Jessie headed right for Collison, who was still sitting on the couch, happily chatting with Dolan. She stomped toward him and stopped inches from his face.

"Stand up," she ordered.

"What the ...?" he started, a confused look on his face.

"Stand up now or I will stand you up," she instructed through gritted teeth.

"I'd do what she suggests," Dolan said, slightly amused.

Murph, on the other hand, didn't look amused at all. Though he didn't step forward or say anything, his right hand was hovering over his sidearm and his body was taut, ready to spring into action.

Collison stood up. Jessie grabbed his arm and twisted it behind his back, pulling out her handcuffs and snapping them onto his wrists in one fluid motion.

"What is going on?" Collison demanded. "What did I do?"

Matilda stepped forward.

"She found some room behind your closet and now she's freaking out about it."

"Yeah, Jett," Jessie agreed. "I'm freaking out. Can you guess why?"

Collison's face turned bright red.

"I can explain," he stammered. "It's not what it seems. I mean, it is. But not in a creepy way."

"You have Claire Stanton's hair in a plastic bin, dude," Jessie reminded him. "It doesn't get creepier than that."

She shoved him down the hall ahead of her before turning back and calling out to Dolan.

102

"Don't let his lackey out of our sight. And call Malibu PD. They should bring their CSU too. There's a piece of clothing that might have blood on it."

Without waiting for a response, she turned around to continue "escorting" Collison out of the house.

*

Jessie waited for someone to call her out.

They were driving back to Central Station. A Malibu PD black-and-white was following them with Collison in the backseat. Their CSU was processing the hidden room. As they'd driven off, Matilda had yelled out to Jett not to say anything. Apparently, in addition to her Perrier-getting skills, she was now an amateur lawyer too.

Having had an hour to calm down, Jessie knew she'd probably overreacted and let her frustration boil over. Part of it was legitimately directed at a guy who may have killed a young woman. But even as she was shoving him ahead of her to the front of the house, some part of her knew this was also misplaced, formless anger about Ryan getting stabbed.

She was helpless to do anything for him. But she could do this. The problem was that by storming out and taking Collison into custody, she'd lost the element of surprise. She could have had Murph keep Matilda away while she peppered the actor with questions about the keepsakes he didn't know she'd found. But now that option was out, he'd be on guard.

They were halfway back to the station when Dolan finally spoke.

"You know," he said, looking straight ahead, "you and your father aren't that different."

She turned to face him, not sure she had heard him correctly.

"What in the goddamn hell do you mean by that?" she demanded.

"I don't mean it as a dig. It's just an observation. You are both relentless in pursuing your goals. In your case, the goal is Claire's killer. In his case, it's you. You both use stealthy techniques to achieve those goals until you determine that a full-on frontal assault is more effective. And you both have terrible impulse control. In your case, that manifests as recklessly arresting a movie star. And in his case, it manifests as murdering people. But you get my point."

She stared at him for a full five seconds before responding.

103

"No, I do not get your point. I am aggressively pursuing a killer, no different than you or any other hard-charging investigator would. Xander Thurman tortures and kills people for fun. I'd say that makes us pretty different, Agent Dolan."

"Well, it's obviously not a perfect comparison," he admitted. "I'm just saying, I can see how you two are related. You both have an intense work ethic, even if his is a little less…evolved."

"I swear to god, if I didn't think I'd get arrested, I would frickin' punch you in the face right now."

"See what I mean about that impulse control?" he said, a smile playing at the edges of his mouth.

Jessie looked out the window. She knew he was screwing with her, trying to lighten the mood a bit after what had been an intense stretch. But she sensed that he still meant what he said, at least a little bit. And because his comment played into her worst fear about herself, it hit her much harder than she knew it was intended to.

She closed her eyes and whispered a familiar mantra to herself.

I am nothing like my father. I am nothing like my father.

CHAPTER EIGHTEEN

Jett Collison did not take Matilda's advice.

After his Miranda rights were read to him, he agreed to talk to Jessie and Dolan without his attorney present. As he settled into a chair in the small conference room, it was clear that he thought he could win them over.

"Let's start with the shrine," Dolan said, beginning the questioning so that Collison wasn't immediately confronted again by Jessie. "What's up with that, Jett?"

"Okay," Collison replied, adjusting his glasses as he spoke. "It's like I tried to tell you before, it's not as bad as it looks."

"It looks pretty bad," Dolan said.

"You can ask Claire. Maybe I kept a few things to remind me of our time together. But I never harassed her or anything. I'm not a stalker."

"What are you then?" Dolan followed up.

"Like I said, I really liked her. I was through with other girls. I was planning to dump that actress I wasn't even really dating. Everyone close to me told me I was making a mistake. Matilda said I was crazy. But I didn't care. So last week I bought a ring and I proposed."

"You asked Claire to marry you?" Jessie asked, incredulous. "What did she say?"

"She said no. She said she wasn't looking to settle down and that it would be weird to go out after that, so she dumped me."

"How did that make you feel?" Jessie asked.

"I was really hurt," he admitted. "I mean, I guess I should have known that she wasn't into that. After all, every guy from that site is rich or powerful. If she had wanted to get married, she had lots of options. But part of me thought she'd see me differently. I'm young. And I guess I thought being famous might make a difference. But she didn't care about that."

"So what did you do when she dumped you?" Dolan asked.

"I used it in my art, man," he replied intently. "I poured all of my heartache into my latest performance. I think I really have a shot at some nominations for this film."

"What's it called?" Dolan asked.

"*I.T. Guy.* It's about this nerdy internet technology employee who wins the heart of his CEO's daughter."

"Sounds like a winner," Jessie said, keeping her comment sarcasm-free. "But are you telling us that her rejection never backed up on you? You just moved on? And remember, Dolan over there is an FBI agent. Lying to him is a federal crime. So think before you reply."

Jett seemed to do exactly that, weighing his next words carefully.

"Listen, I'm not saying I handled everything perfectly—obviously not. I mean, you found the tub of hair. There was the photo album, although I'd bet there are a lot of people who collect photos of their exes."

"Including naked ones taken without her knowledge kept in a secret room?" Jessie wondered.

"Okay, that part doesn't look great, I admit. But I wasn't thinking clearly at the time. I was super messed up, emotions-wise. I'm sure you'll find other stuff too. I'll confess to you right now that I found out she had gone out with an executive at a studio I've worked for and I told them I'd never make another movie there unless they fired him. I mean, that clearly wasn't cool. But it's not stalker-y."

"Yeah, it kind of is," countered Jessie.

"Did Claire press charges or something? Is she complaining? Because I don't think she even knows about any of this stuff."

"Not even the scarf with her blood on it?" Dolan asked, notably ignoring Collison's question.

"Blood?" Collison repeated, stunned. "That's not blood. It's lipstick. She got it on her scarf and said it was ruined so she tossed it out. I kept part of it, sure. But it's not blood."

Jessie and Dolan looked at each other. That claim would be verified or disproven soon. But Collison was looking less viable as a suspect with each passing second.

"Why did you think it was blood?" he asked, his voice rising. "Has something happened to her?"

106

Jessie could sense they were losing him and tried to get in one last question that had been eating at her before he completely lost it.

"Jett," she said firmly, "you said Matilda thought you were crazy to propose to Claire. Did she seem upset about it?"

"I don't know," Jett said answered, increasingly agitated. "I don't really pay attention to my assistant's moods. You didn't answer my question—has something happened to Claire?"

They couldn't stall any longer and Jessie was curious to see Jett's reaction when they told him information he theoretically didn't already know. She glanced over at Dolan, who nodded slightly, giving her the go-ahead.

"She's dead, Jett," she said flatly. "She was murdered."

"What? No!"

His brow was furrowed as if he'd just been asked a tough math question he couldn't answer. He looked from her to Dolan, who nodded in confirmation. He looked back at Jessie, as if hoping she might change her mind.

"For real?" he asked plaintively.

"For real," Jessie assured him, still unable to tell whether he was sincere or not. Forget *I.T. Guy*. If he was faking it, this was easily his best performance.

"When?"

"The night before last," she said. "That's why Agent Dolan was asking you where you were then. And I noticed from his notes you didn't have a very good answer."

"You think I did this?" Collison asked, his eyes wide.

"We're trying to eliminate you as a suspect, Jett," she said supportively. "But it's hard when, according to the notes I'm reading, you say that two nights ago you forgot your phone at the studio and hitchhiked back to get it because your car broke down."

"But it's true. The studio usually assigns me a driver. But by the time I realized I'd left my phone there, he was gone. And I don't drive much so I didn't know my car battery had died."

"But you see the problem, Jett," she said calmly. "We can't trace your whereabouts using your vehicle because you didn't drive it. You didn't rideshare so we can't track that either."

"How was I supposed to call a Lyft without my phone?" he interrupted.

"But you didn't call a cab either, which would have made sense. You hitched a ride into town from Malibu?"

107

"I used to do it all the time before I got famous. And a cab would have taken forever to get to my place."

"But that means no one can vouch for you. Why didn't you ask Matilda? I'm sure she would have driven you."

"It was her night off. She lives in Culver City. I didn't want to bother her to come all the way out to get me in Malibu and take me into Hollywood. That would have taken her hours."

"Very thoughtful of you," Jessie said. "So to review, we can't use your phone to locate you because you left it at work. We can't track your vehicle because you didn't use it. You took an unverifiable method of transit to get your phone. That means that you were off the grid for about two hours, including the window when Claire was murdered."

"It's just a terrible coincidence," he insisted.

"Maybe," she said.

"It's true. Can't you check video cameras?"

"What, you mean all the security cameras the city posts on random, unpopulated stretches of the Pacific coastline? That's not a thing, Jett."

He looked like he wanted to reply but then stopped. He was at a loss. It didn't matter because just then Decker poked his head in.

"Can I speak to you two?" he asked Jessie and Dolan.

"Sure," she said and then to Collison, "stay put."

"Where am I gonna go?" he moaned.

Jessie almost chuckled as she walked to the door. She didn't know if this guy was guilty but she was enjoying tying him in knots. When she, Dolan, and Murph stepped out into the hall, the expression on Decker's face told her she needed to get serious.

"What is it?" she asked.

"Preliminary results came back on the scarf. The red mark was lipstick. You have to cut Collison loose."

CHAPTER NINETEEN

Jessie wasn't shocked.

Each new piece of information had made her less and less confident that the actor was their guy. And despite crushing him moments ago for his total lack of an alibi, she just couldn't bring herself to buy that he was the perpetrator of this crime.

To her surprise, Decker disagreed.

"We're going to have him tailed once he gets out," he said with an edge in his voice. "We can't keep him any more without causing a meltdown at headquarters. But if he makes a mistake when he's out, we'll be all over it."

"You really think he's our guy?" Jessie asked, thrown by his certainty.

"Hunt, I may not be a profiler. But the guy had a secret shrine to a woman he'd just proposed to, a woman who turned him down. And he has no alibi for the time of death. I mean, he literally cannot provide a scintilla of proof of his whereabouts. This guy isn't getting off scot-free just because his smile makes people weak in the knees. Celebrity is not a passport to criminality."

"It kind of seems like it is," Dolan said drily.

Decker had to take a deep breath to keep his cool at the FBI agent's snarky comment.

"Look, the powers that be don't want a lawsuit if this guy ends up being innocent. And truthfully, I'm happy to avoid the media attention as long as possible. It protects the investigation. And it protects Hunt. Once word gets out that Jett Collision was arrested, how long after that do you think it will be before her name leaks too? That's the last thing we need."

"I'm with the captain on that one," Murph added quietly.

Decker seemed happy to have the support.

"If this guy is guilty, he's going down, no matter who he is," he said. "So let him go. But don't stop looking. We're one more piece of evidence away from re-arresting him. If we take him down, I want it to be airtight."

"Yes sir," Jessie said as he walked off.

She turned to Dolan, who looked as skeptical as she felt.

"I get equal justice for everyone," she said to him when the captain was out of earshot. "But the question is: do we actually think he's guilty?"

Dolan sighed heavily.

"I don't know, Hunt. On paper, this guy is a slam dunk, based on everything the captain just said. But my gut says he doesn't feel right."

"Me either," she agreed before adding, "Of course, sometimes my gut gets me in trouble. I'm trying to rely less on it and more on the evidence."

Murph, silent as usual beside them, perked up suddenly. He turned away and spoke into his comm. Dolan, who hadn't noticed, replied.

"I don't know. In my experience, for people like us, the evidence is secondary. We solve cases based on our ability to read people. I know that's counter to all the training. But I think it's true. When it comes down to proof or gut, I'll go with what's in my hairy belly every time."

Murph waved at Jessie to get her attention.

"You've got a call," he said. "It's from Detective Hernandez. It's being patched through to my phone. You can take it in the closet across the way."

Jessie looked at Dolan.

"You mind?" she asked.

"Of course not," he said. "I'll coordinate letting Collison out and see what Decker has planned in the way of surveillance."

"Okay," she agreed. "When I get back, I think we should go back to the drawing board. We can't pursue this guy more aggressively without something firm to connect him. So we should go back through the other texts from clients on the site to see if we missed anything."

"That sounds fun."

"It's what my gut recommends," she said.

"I've got Hernandez on the line," Murph interrupted, handing her the phone.

She took it, stepped into the small closet that was becoming her second office, and pretended not to notice the butterflies flitting around in her stomach.

She'd managed to successfully force Ryan from her mind while investigating Collison. But now, with him conscious and ready to talk, all her confused emotions reared up again. She put the phone to her ear and spoke.

"I can't leave you alone for a second," she said, feigning anger.

"I know, right?" he replied. His voice sounded weak and distant.

"How are you doing?" she asked, unable to keep up the charade of light banter.

"Peachy," he answered raspily. "They say I'm getting transferred downtown to California Hospital Medical Center later today. It's less than two miles from the station so it'll be easier to provide security for me."

"Good to know," she said. "That'll make it easier to visit you. But it doesn't really tell me how you're doing."

"I've been better," he admitted. "But the doctor says I get another hit of pain medication in a couple minutes, so I've got that going for me, which is nice."

"It sounds like you could use it now."

"I didn't want to get fuzzy before I spoke to you," he said earnestly.

"I appreciate that. So maybe while you're clear-headed you can tell me how you're really doing rather than repeatedly avoiding the question."

There was a pause on the other end of the line. For a moment, Jessie thought he was debating whether to update her. But then she heard a loud gulp and realized he was struggling to catch his breath.

"I'll be okay," he finally said. "My arm is all stitched up. The knife didn't get anything vital. And it's not my shooting hand, so there's that. They were worried about the jab to the stomach for a while. But it missed everything vital too. Mostly just got belly fat."

"You don't have any belly fat," Jessie pointed out.

"I'm trying to be self-deprecating here," he wheezed. "Anyway, the doctors say I was incredibly lucky; that I should be back at work in a month and cleared for field duty in two."

"That's great," Jessie said. "But why do I sense that you don't think your quick recovery is luck-based."

"I think we both already know the answer to that one, Jessie."

"Because that's what my father wanted," she said resignedly.

"That's what your dad wanted," he confirmed.

"You didn't 'fend him off' like Decker said?"

111

"I wish I could claim that. But he completely surprised me. The first slice came before I even knew he was there. The second one was more me throwing my arm at him than him swinging at me. I was on the ground before I really knew what was happening."

"And the gunshot?" she asked. "You didn't hit him?"

"I wasn't even firing at him. He was gone by the time I pulled my weapon out. I shot in the air as a plea for help because I couldn't manage to yell."

"Well, his little plan didn't work," she said, trying to buck him up. "We realized he was using you to get to me, hoping I'd show up at the hospital so he could take me down. I'm sorry. I would have come. But everyone agreed it would be a mistake."

"That's okay," he said, his voice fading so that she had to concentrate to hear him. "You made the right call. But that's not the only reason he let me live."

"What do you mean?"

There was a long pause so she repeated the question.

"What do you mean it wasn't the only reason, Ryan?"

"What?" he said hazily. "Oh, sorry, I think the doctor gave me the pain meds without telling me. I'm feeling...cloudy. What was your question again?"

"Why did Xander Thurman let you live?"

"He wanted me to give you a massage. I mean...a message."

"What's the message, Ryan?"

"He said to tell you: You're wrong. Look again."

"That's it? That's all he said?"

But Ryan didn't answer. Instead, she heard a long slow, wheezy breath. He was asleep.

CHAPTER TWENTY

Jessie decided to keep the message to herself.

Until she better understood what it meant, there was no point freaking everyone else out about it.

Back in the conference room, Collison was gone and Dolan was poring over old text messages from the Look of Love website. When she came in, he looked up.

"Everything okay?" he asked.

"Yep," she said. "He's on the mend—should be back in the thick of it in a couple of months."

"Want to talk about it?" he asked.

"Not really," she answered honestly.

"Good, because I could use a jumpstart here," he said. "If we're both skeptical that Collison is our guy, despite the strikes against him, then we're really scraping the bottom of the barrel for legitimate suspects."

"That was my thought earlier too before I found that bin under Collison's bed. I was dreading the possibility of having to wade through all this crap again to see if we missed anything. When I found that stuff, I thought my prayers had been answered. And then, when Matilda caught me, I thought I'd better say my prayers, she scared me so bad."

"Yeah, she's an odd duck," he agreed.

Jessie sat down next to him, allowing a thought to percolate in her brain for a few seconds."

"Just how odd a duck do you think she is?" she finally asked.

"What—you think this was her?" Dolan asked.

"I'm just saying," she began, "she's obviously in love with Jett Collison. She wouldn't have loved it when he started to take Claire seriously, much less when he proposed."

"But Claire said no so she was no longer a threat."

"In theory," Jessie agreed. "But Jett was still pining, dare I say obsessing over her. If anybody would have known about that shrine in the secret room, it was Matilda. If she found it, it couldn't have

113

made her happy. How do we know she didn't kill Claire in a fit of jealous rage? How do we know she didn't mess with Jett's phone that night—or his car battery for that matter—to screw with his alibi? She punishes him for loving someone else by framing him for killing her. Then she comes in at the last minute to rescue him, earning his endless devotion."

"How does she do that?" Dolan wanted to know.

"I don't know. Maybe she finds video footage of him that verifies his alibi?"

"Isn't that our job?"

"Yes. But if she set him up, she'd know exactly where to find the footage that saves him. Do we even know what her alibi is? Where was she two nights ago?"

Murph coughed self-consciously from the corner of the room. Jessie looked up at him. It was obvious he had something to say.

"Yes?" she asked.

"While you we upstairs in that mansion violating Collison's privacy and Dolan was interrogating the guy, Matilda came back with that water looking for you. I knew you were up to no good so I tried to stall her. In the course of that stalling attempt, I asked about her life and stuff. She mentioned that she was starring in a play in Rolling Hills. She performed two nights ago. It started at nine p.m. and ran for two hours. "

Jessie was silent for a moment, letting the information sink in.

"Has anyone checked this alibi?" she finally asked.

"I believe Toomey mentioned it to your captain when you two were questioning Collison. He was having someone follow up."

"Rolling Hills is really far from Studio City," Dolan said, almost apologetically. "The chances of her getting there after performing onstage are remote."

"Yeah, I can do the math on that," Jessie said tersely before turning back to Murph. "Why do I suspect you've already 'followed up'?"

"I may have checked online to see if there was any footage of her performing."

"And?" Jessie asked expectantly.

"A couple of people recorded it on YouTube. I'm not sure why. The play isn't very good. And Matilda is...perhaps better suited to her day job."

"How long were you going to let me go on like that, spouting off totally bogus theories?"

"For a while longer," Murph said. "They weren't awful theories. And it was pretty entertaining."

Jessie slumped back in her chair, too deflated to chew him out. Once again she'd let her instincts take over before even checking to see if the evidence bore it out. Despite Dolan's embrace of the "gut method," it didn't seem to be serving her very well lately.

She resolved to spend the next few hours focused only on leads based on credible facts, even if that meant going through dozens of mind-numbing texts from sexually rapacious old guys and the young women who were playing them.

And that's exactly what she did. Over the remainder of the afternoon, she reviewed hundreds of texts, looking for anything even mildly relevant. Nothing she read was out of the ordinary. Actually, that wasn't quite true. Some of the messages in other threads were sexually graphic. Some were depraved. Some were cruel. But none of the messages to or from Claire was threatening or even especially titillating. The word that best described them was "businesslike."

As she studied them, she couldn't stop her thoughts from drifting to the message Ryan had passed along from her father: You're wrong. Look again.

What does that mean? And why is he saying it?

She knew that she should be more focused on the second question. After all, the first one was bait intended to draw her in. And yet, that first question was what intrigued her more.

Did he mean she was wrong about this case? If so, how could he even know that she was investigating it? Was he somehow following her? Had he, despite the best efforts of the marshals, managed to keep tabs on her movements, just as Crutchfield had?

An idea occurred to her. She clicked through the LAPD's intranet site until she got to the page for the media tracking unit, which kept logs of every reference to an LAPD case in local media. She typed out a quick request before returning to her thoughts.

Assuming Xander did somehow know about the case, how could he know she was wrong about her assumptions without access to the evidence? The answer to that didn't take long. Xander Thurman, she reminded herself, wasn't an evidence guy. Like Agent Dolan, he was a gut guy. He used his instincts and knowledge of human nature to make his moves.

Unfortunately those moves usually involve killing people. But they also involved knowing how people might put themselves in vulnerable positions that would make killing them easier. It was a sick, bastardized variation of what a profiler did, but used the same basic skill set.

Setting aside the discomfort of recognizing once again that she and her father weren't that different in how they approached their "work," she tried to home in on what about the people involved in this case would make Xander think she was wrong to pursue them as she had.

He didn't know any of the details of Claire's life so that wasn't the source of his comment. All he knew was what was publicly available—that an attractive young party girl had been stabbed to death and that, based on interviews with some friends and social media photos, she was known to have dated several older, wealthy men.

And then it hit her. Xander didn't need to know anything about Claire. He just needed to know how the mind of her killer worked. And he was an expert at that. Then again, so was she.

So what would motivate this killer? What incorrect assumption am I making?

For starters, all the likely suspects were rich men trying to keep these relationships on the down low.

Are they though?

Now that she thought about it, that wasn't really the case. The three main suspects she'd questioned were all wealthy, powerful men. But none of them would be truly ruined if word of their involvement with Claire got out.

Milton Jerebko had told his wife, Gayle, about the affair before Claire died. And he didn't seem overly concerned about potential voters finding out. That's why Claire's blackmail scheme had failed.

Gunther Stroud had an open relationship with his wife, who didn't even live in the same country as him. The idea that he could be shamed by the revelation of a relationship with a young hottie seemed absurd.

Even Jett Collison, with his fake actress girlfriend, wasn't hiding Claire from those closest to him. And having proposed, he had to know that if she said yes, the truth of how they met would get out. He clearly wasn't overly concerned about it. Besides, he had seemed genuinely distraught over her death. And he just wasn't that great an actor to be faking it.

The simple truth was that none of those suspects had a reason to kill her. The people in their lives either already knew about Claire or wouldn't have been shocked to hear about her. None of these guys would have viewed the potential scandal of being associated with her as remotely worth the risk of killing her.

So either the killer was someone they hadn't found yet who *would* fear being exposed or there was another motive for the killing. And since Jessie had gone through every text from every suitor on the site, she knew there weren't any legitimate "fear of exposure" candidates left.

That left the alternate motive theory. And Jessie was fairly confident she knew what that motive was: passion twisted into rage. She'd already theorized that the use of keys as the murder weapon suggested the killing wasn't premeditated. If it were, the killer would have used a more efficient, less messy implement. The decision to kill was made in the moment, without thought of the consequences. This was a crime born out of passion, not fear.

For the first time in hours, Jessie felt like she was on the right track.

Focus on the passion, find the killer.

CHAPTER TWENTY ONE

So who had that kind of passion?

Jessie thought again of Matilda, who clearly carried a torch for Jett and might have let her jealousy get out of control. But even she likely would have brought some kind of weapon with her to a confrontation. Besides, she had an unassailable alibi.

Jessie started to go back through the suspects she'd reviewed previously to look at them through this new prism of passion rather than fear. Just then an email alert popped up on her laptop. It was from the Media Tracking Unit. The message was a single line:

"One media engagement found one requested matter, with relevant video."

The video was attached. She opened it. Immediately, a news hit from a local station began to play. It was from yesterday, detailing the sad death of a young woman in the Studio City home she rented. As footage from the scene played, the voiceover said the police weren't commenting but her roommate confirmed that the woman was stabbed to death.

Just before the reporter's concluding standup, there was a small clip of B-roll showing several investigators walking around inside the house. The glare from the window made it hard to see much detail. The camera zoomed in to get a better view. It was still hard to discern identities. But one of the investigators was a tall brunette with her hair in a ponytail. If someone already knew what she looked like, they would easily be able to identify her as Jessie Hunt. Clearly, Xander Thurman had been watching and done just that.

Equipped with that information and the address of the house, it wouldn't have been hard for him to have learned the victim's identity, find the LOL site, hire or threaten someone to hack it, and read the same texts she had, ultimately drawing his own conclusion as to the killer's identity.

If he was on the side of the angels, we could actually use his skills.

The dark irony that her father would have made a pretty good profiler made her smile slightly before she got serious again. She had to assume, based on this new knowledge, that her father wasn't just blowing smoke and really did know who killed Claire. So she could take as credible his words to Ryan: "You're wrong. Look again."

That answered her first question: What does that mean?

Of course her second question—why is he saying it—still hung over her like a cloud threatening to open into a downpour. But for now, she chose to ignore it.

Armed with something approaching certainty, she went back through the suspects, looking for anyone who might be motivated by passion. But still, there was nothing. Well, not quite nothing. She did notice something odd that she'd missed before.

In one of the text exchanges between Claire and Milton Jerebko, several weeks after they'd clearly been seeing each other, he asked for her email address. She gave it in her next reply. There was no other reference to the request in future texts, which continued for weeks until the whole blackmail thing reared its head.

Why ask for her email address and then keep communicating via texts on the app? It didn't seem to make any sense.

"Hey," she said, looking up at Dolan and speaking to him for the first time in what felt like hours.

"Yeah?" he replied, his own eyes bleary from constant, close reading.

"Did we ever look at Claire's email exchanges?"

"I didn't know people her age still even used email," he replied only half-joking.

She ignored the crack and pressed ahead.

"In one text, Jerebko asks her for it and she gives it to him. But then they keep texting. I would have thought they'd have switched over to email exclusively at that point. But they kept chatting on the app as if nothing had changed."

Dolan rifled through some papers until he found what he was looking for. He held up a single sheet.

"It looks like your tech unit got her email password from the provider and sent it to us. But everybody has been so busy that it looks like no one has actually gone through the messages yet. Why do you ask?"

"I'm curious to see if they ever actually communicated off-app."

"Well, have at it," he said, handing her the page as he stood up. "I'm going to go shake the dew off the lily if you know what I mean."

"No idea, Dolan," she replied, scowling. "You're very cryptic."

"I'm saying I'm going to the restroom to urinate," he said in a tone that suggested he was extremely proud of himself. He managed to just get out the door before getting nailed by the pen she threw at him.

Refocusing, she plugged the password into Claire's email account and pulled up her inbox. She went to the date of the text when Jerebko first asked for her email address and searched for any messages that seemed related. One titled "Re: LOL" seemed to fit the bill. She opened and read the email.

It took physical effort to prevent her jaw from dropping at what she saw.

She looked over at Murph out of the corner of her eye. He was oblivious to her, scrolling through his phone as he stood in the corner of the room. She opened the next message in the exchange and nearly gasped. Each subsequent message gave her a little internal jolt that required concerted effort not to display.

When she reached the final message, Jessie leaned back in her chair. Her mind was racing. What she saw was provocative and potentially game-changing. But as she sat quietly, trying to look normal, she realized that if she told Dolan, he'd want to pursue it in the standard G-man fashion, coming in hard and fast.

But if Jessie's instincts were right, that wouldn't work. The way to get to the truth in this case required something more subtle—the kind of manipulation that Dolan wasn't capable of. But she was.

The only problem was that if she showed up with him and her marshals in tow, there was no way she could get to the truth. She needed to be alone, to create a sense of security for her prey; to make the subject think that she was there to help rather than catch.

And that required her to get out of this station and away from the men who were assigned to protect her. She couldn't show up with a coterie of feds. She needed to look trustworthy. And that meant looking vulnerable. And the only way to appear vulnerable was, on some level, to actually *be* vulnerable.

"Hey, Murph," she said, making the marshal look up reluctantly from his phone. "I've got to shake the dew off the lily. Be back in a few."

He didn't even smile as she got up and walked out. She glanced back to make sure he wasn't watching. He wasn't. She also noticed her sidearm was resting on the table beside her laptop and briefly considered going back for it. But that would definitely draw Murph's attention and suspicion. Instead, she hurried down the hall, not wanting to bump into Dolan along the way.

By the time the FBI agent and the US marshal began to get suspicious, she had already requisitioned a department vehicle. By the time they started looking for her, she was on the road and en route to the West Hollywood Hills home of Milton Jerebko.

CHAPTER TWENTY TWO

Jessie knew she didn't have long.

As she drove up the sharply winding hill streets, she did the math in her head. It would have taken about five minutes for Murph to start to get suspicious; maybe another two or three before he acted on it and checked on her. And then maybe two more before he concluded that she was genuinely gone. So call it ten minutes to be conservative before he began actively searching for her.

He'd check her phone signal. She'd turned off the location sharing feature and the phone itself. But that was only a stopgap measure. They'd be able to ping her GPS location as soon as they got the system active. That wouldn't take more than five minutes, knowing him.

They'd be frustrated when they realized her phone's signal was coming from inside the station conference room. But that would only be a temporary setback. They'd learn about her vehicle requisition pretty fast. When they did, they'd pinpoint where it was using the signal beacon all LAPD vehicles were equipped with. That whole process might take a total of five additional minutes.

And she was sure that as soon as Murph saw the direction she was going, he'd guess her destination and send West Hollywood PD to meet her. So best-case scenario: she had a twenty-minute head start, realistically closer to fifteen. That wasn't a lot of time for what she had in mind.

When she arrived, the gate was open, which seemed to defeat the purpose of the high stone walls but made her life easier. She zipped up the Jerebko driveway, parked, and jogged the last few steps to their front door porch. She was about to ring the doorbell when she saw movement to her left in the shadows by a tree in their yard.

She pivoted in that direction and reached for her gun. It wasn't there. She remembered she'd had to leave it on the table in the conference room. The figure near the tree stepped into the dull glow of the porch light.

It was Crutchfield.

"Greetings, Miss Jessie," he said lazily, as if he didn't have a care in the world.

Jessie didn't know how to react. Mixed in with the fear at his presence was her surprise that he was able to know this was her destination and get here first.

None of that matters now.

Without her service weapon, Jessie recognized she had no clear advantage. She was actually taller than him and in better shape. But as she'd learned in the ladies' room bar the previous night, he was shockingly strong. And she didn't know if he was armed. His right hand rested at his side but his left was noticeably held behind his back.

She did still have the extra pistol she kept in her concealed ankle holster. But it wasn't designed for quick, easy access. By the time she reached down, unholstered it, got it out, and pointed it in his direction, he'd likely have time to shoot her, physically attack her, or get away. She had to think of a different way out of this.

"Two visits in two nights," she said, trying to match his unhurried manner. "If you're not careful, people will think you're courting me, Mr. Crutchfield."

"I would never be so presumptuous, Miss Jessie," he replied, smiling broadly, even as his fingers twitched slightly, like a gunfighter anticipating a duel.

"Are you here to finish what you started?" she asked, trying to seem engaged even as she desperately tried to think of how to get the upper hand. It wasn't lost on her that despite his leisurely manner and southern drawl, Bolton Crutchfield was a brutal serial killer.

"You're hurting my feelings, Miss Jessie," he said, his lips pursing into a mock pout. "All I did last night was warn you of an imminent threat to your safety."

"A threat which never materialized," she shot back.

"Likely because of my warning," he countered.

"And you didn't only warn me," she reminded him. "You also slammed my head against a mirror and knocked me out. Or did you forget that part?"

"I had to extricate myself from the situation quickly. Your Murphy marshal man was getting antsy."

"Still, not very gentlemanly."

"Touché," he acknowledged.

Jessie tried to stay focused, calculating her options. She didn't seem to have many. Once again she thought of the pistol at her ankle. And once again she determined that at his distance from her, he would either escape or be on her before she could access it.

Meanwhile, time was ticking away. Every second she bantered with him was one less to interrogate the murder suspect inside before the cops arrived. Crutchfield smiled again, as if he understood her dilemma.

"I can see you're torn, Miss Jessie. This is a real pickle, isn't it?"

Irked at his teasing, she decided to cut to the chase.

"What do you want, Crutchfield? If you're not here to kill me, you must have another reason. Please just spit it out, because, in case you couldn't tell, I'm a little busy right now."

The smile remained plastered to his face but his eyes lost their gleam and went cold.

"You are such a party pooper, Miss Jessie. And so ungrateful, what with me here to help you *again*."

"Then help, Bolton," she said curtly, using his first name to emphasize her point. "I'm tired of these games."

He looked down for a moment, as if he'd lost a bit of self-control and was trying to find it again. When he looked up again, the mask had returned.

"With your harsh tone, you are making it quite hard for me to continue in the role of your guardian angel. And your repeated half-glances at your ankle are quite unsettling. I have important information for you, Miss Jessie. But I can only share it if I have assurances that you're not going to try to reach for that pistol by your shoe. Can you give me that assurance?"

"How about I assure you that once I pull out that pistol and arrest you, you'll do your talking down at the station?"

Crutchfield smiled at her as if she was a small child demanding to be taken for ice cream.

"I think we both know," he said in his maddeningly soothing manner, "that that is the least likely outcome of our interaction. Trying would put you at physical risk. Even if you could pull it off, we both know that's not really what you want. If I'm taken into custody, I won't be sharing what I know. And what I know could be very useful to you the next time you run into your father, whose intentions toward you aren't nearly as benevolent as mine. You have a decision to make, Miss Jessie."

She did indeed. She could try to make a move for the gun. But every instinct she had told her that would end badly. She could continue to chat up the guy in the hopes that the cavalry would show up and get him. But he wasn't dumb enough to stick around that long. And even if he did, that would sabotage all the work she'd done to get here and question the Jerebkos *before* the police interrupted. Finally, even if Crutchfield deigned to be arrested, she suspected he wasn't bluffing. He wouldn't say a word about her father, just to spite her.

So when it came down to it, there wasn't really any choice at all.

"You have my word," she said reluctantly. "I won't go for the pistol unless you make an aggressive move. Now what do you know?"

He was just about to reply when Jessie heard a voice on the other side of the door and glanced in that direction.

"Who is it?" Gayle Jerebko called out. She must have heard them talking.

Jessie looked back at Crutchfield. Ever so slowly, with a huge grin on his face, he took his index finger and traced a small circle on the right side of his forehead.

"Who's there?" Gayle repeated.

"It's Jessie Hunt. I need to speak to your husband."

As she waited for a response, she and the escaped serial killer stared silently at each other.

"Hold on," Gayle said. Jessie heard her undoing the locks.

A second later, the door opened and Jessie turned to see Gayle Martindale Jerebko, dressed in what looked to be a silk kimono.

"Please come in," she said in a surprisingly pleasant tone.

Jessie glanced back to her left. But all that stood there now was the tree. Crutchfield had vanished.

CHAPTER TWENTY THREE

"What is this all about?" Milton Jerebko demanded angrily.

Gayle had just led Jessie into the living room, where her mind was still reeling from what had just happened outside. She hadn't had time to process what Crutchfield's gesture meant when Jerebko stormed in, red-faced and fuming.

"At least let the woman sit down," Gayle chastised, motioning for Jessie to take a seat on the couch.

The Crutchfield encounter had rattled her to the point that she wasn't acting shaken. She was really feeling it.

Use that, Jessie. Get your game face on. You can deal with what just happened later. Right now, you have a job to do.

She wanted to appear harmless and nonthreatening and decided to channel her current uncertainty into the task at hand.

"I just have a few more questions," she said meekly, following Gayle's lead and sitting gingerly on the couch.

"Because of you and your LAPD buddies, my world is in shambles!" Jerebko shouted.

"What do you mean, sir?" Jessie asked, regrouping slightly. "I thought you'd already told your wife about the affair and that your constituents would be understanding."

Jerebko stopped for a second, clearly not expecting that response.

"Yes, well, it turns out that repairing a marriage after admitting an infidelity is made doubly difficult when the media pores over every detail of that infidelity. And while my constituents are understanding of flawed politicians, they don't love having their noses rubbed in it. And then there are the kids."

"Yes," Gayle agreed, "this has been very hard on the children."

Jessie turned her attention to her, trying to look calm and not like she had between five and ten minutes to prove her theory.

"What about you, Mrs. Jerebko? This can't be easy, trying to keep a stiff upper lip, dealing with the indignity caused by your husband's inability to control his middle-aged infatuation."

"Hey!" Jerebko protested.

"You're handling it a lot better than I would have," Jessie continued, ignoring Milton as she gave her full attention to Gayle. "You know, when I found out my husband was having an affair, it was all I could do not to bump off his mistress. Of course, he ended up doing that himself and trying to frame me for it. So…totally different situation. Still, I feel for you."

"Thank you," Gayle replied carefully.

"I mean, it's hard to fathom the arrogance," Jessie said, warming up. "I don't want to project my situation onto your own. But in both cases, we're talking about narcissistic men who think they're entitled to everything. Your husband believes he's entitled to have the voters' forgiveness. He believes he should be able to maintain his marriage to you and have a relationship with some young sex toy. He thinks that you and your children should just accept his bad judgment and move on, without any consequences."

"What the hell…?" Milton tried to interject but Jessie rolled right over him.

"I'll bet it never even occurred to him how you might feel," she continued. "That you might feel shame at being treated so poorly by your own husband. That you might feel anger at this young woman who blew up your seemingly happy life. And most of all, the constant frustration you must feel at knowing your life isn't as happy as it seems from the outside."

"I'm not sure what you mean," Gayle said, though her eyes suggested otherwise.

"Oh, come on, Gayle. As long as we're laying it all out on the table, let's be honest about this as well. Milton's not the only one who deserves some passion in his life, right? You're entitled to feel those things again too. And if he can't provide it, I bet part of you thought maybe you should divorce his sorry ass and find someone who can appreciate all the effort you've put into looking the way you look for him. You can't tell me it never occurred to you."

Gayle was silent, her jaw muscles tight.

"Gayle," Milton said indignantly. "Tell this woman that her insinuations are insulting."

Jessie ignored him and looked deep into Gayle's eyes. She saw the pain and the resentment there and she knew it was time.

"You could have divorced this sorry excuse for a man, Gayle," she said softly, almost in a whisper. "But you went a different way, didn't you?"

"Excuse me?" Gayle said, uncrossing and recrossing her legs, making the kimono swish slightly.

"I mean, when you confronted Claire, you probably thought you might end up killing her. But you didn't expect it to go the way it did, right?"

Gayle's mouth dropped open. Milton looked totally confused.

"What are you talking about?" he asked.

"Oh, didn't Gayle tell you?" Jessie said, feigning surprise.

"Tell me what?"

"That she found out about your affair weeks before you admitted it."

Milton stared at Gayle, who only gulped. Jessie pressed on.

"You really should do a better job of clearing your internet history, Milton. The site came right up when Gayle borrowed your laptop one day. You can imagine her shock when she saw how you were spending your spare time."

"Is this true?" he demanded of his wife.

"Are you really the one who should be asking questions?" Jessie chastised him, then turned back to Gayle. "You were all ready to rip her to shreds, weren't you, after you pretended to be your husband and sent that email asking her to meet you? But then, when you were with her in person, she wasn't what you expected, was she?"

Gayle didn't respond, didn't even nod. But she didn't stop Jessie either, which reassured her that the on-the-fly psychological profile she'd developed about the woman wasn't far off. So she went on.

"Whatever you originally had in mind faded away when you talked to her, didn't it, Gayle? You saw what it was in her that made Milton lose his head—because you did the same thing. You went to that meeting with bad intent and somewhere along the way, you fell for her. Am I right, Gayle?"

Gayle nodded ever so slightly.

"It's okay," Jessie assured her. "That's not a crime. Who could have known that your husband's mistress would fill such an emotional and physical hole in your life? Somehow, you ended up cheating on your husband with his own mistress. It's almost poetic justice."

Milton's mouth was agape. Gayle glanced over at him with a mix of guilt and pride.

"You didn't deserve her," she muttered.

"No, he didn't," Jessie agreed, not wanting to lose control of the situation. "But you did. You were much smarter about your trysts than he was, weren't you? No more online contact after you started seeing her. You called her from pay phones instead of your cell, using different ones every time. You were careful. This relationship was becoming important to you and you didn't want it be discovered by the kind of sloppiness that undid Milton."

"Only for a little while longer," Gayle said through gritted teeth. "I was going to dump him—let him squirm."

"And he would have too," Jessie noted. "I checked. You have a pre-nup. Doesn't it say something about him getting nothing if the marriage dissolves on account of infidelity? If Claire stayed quiet about the two of you, you could have left him in the cold and then turned around and been with her. Wouldn't that have been sweet?"

"It would have," Gayle agreed, her eyes going soft at the thought of it.

"But something went wrong, didn't it?" Jessie said, bringing things back to the present. She was keenly aware that time was running short. Any moment, the sound of approaching sirens might shut things down just as they were getting interesting.

Gayle again nodded without speaking.

"Let me guess. You professed your love to her. She pulled back; said she wasn't interested in a serious relationship. She was young and single and wanted to keep it that way. She didn't love you."

"She was more diplomatic than that," Gayle said, crossing her legs again, this time more quickly. The swishing of the silk sounded like a snake scurrying through long grass. "But when it came down to it, yes, she dumped me."

How did that make you feel?" Jessie asked in her best therapist voice.

"Not great, obviously."

"It was a little more than that though, wasn't it, Gayle? You couldn't let it go. Those emails started up again, even though they put your secret at risk. I read them all. You pleaded with her; offered to set her up so she'd never have to work again. But she never even responded, did she?"

Gayle's icy stare was answer enough. Jessie pressed on, knowing she was in the home stretch.

"And then she went and blackmailed Milton. But you knew it was directed as much at you as at him. You knew that was her unspoken way of hinting that he better pay up or else your secrets would come out too. It probably felt almost as if the blackmail of your husband was intended to deliberately hurt *you* more than him."

"I didn't feel that way," Gayle corrected her. "It *was* that way."

"So you went to see her one more time, at her place, feeling wounded and angry and betrayed—hoping to get her to reconsider. Not just the blackmail, but to reconsider the two of you as well. But she wasn't having any of it. Maybe she was less diplomatic this time around. She probably had no idea what a wronged, gym-fit forty-something woman was capable of when pushed to the edge. She underestimated you, didn't she, Gayle? She dismissed you. And that was one time too many. So you grabbed the only thing you had at that moment that could express the fury you felt—your keys."

Gayle remained silent, staring back at her. Jessie studied the woman's expression and was surprised that the best description of it was...appreciative. It was as if Gayle Martindale Jerebko was thankful that someone finally understood her.

"You jammed them in her throat, didn't you, Gayle?" Jessie said, leading her where she knew the woman wanted to go. "You let her know you weren't going to be ignored anymore. How did that feel?"

She went quiet, waiting for Gayle's response. Next to his wife, Milton sat, limp and stunned. Finally Gayle opened her mouth.

"I felt free, maybe for the first time ever."

CHAPTER TWENTY FOUR

"Gayle, shut up!" Milton shouted, suddenly snapping out of his daze. "She's trying to get you to confess. Don't say another word."

"It's too late, Milton," Gayle said casually. "She obviously already knows everything. She has the emails. She'll check everywhere I've been. There's no point in pretending."

"But knowing something and proving it are different things," he protested. "Don't make it easy. We'll get you a good lawyer. There's still hope."

Gayle turned to him with an almost pitying look.

"Hope for what—our marriage? You've already destroyed that. Our kids are already ashamed that you're their father. What's a little more material for their therapy sessions? So she knows? It was worth it, if only to ruin you, you selfish bastard."

Milton looked at her in uncomprehending horror. After a moment he blinked and stood up.

"I need a drink," he said and shuffled off to the kitchen.

Jessie watched him go and turned back to his wife.

"Gayle, you did the right thing coming clean," she said. "I recently had a case where the perpetrator was a woman not unlike you. I determined her guilt and asked her to give up. It was a crime of passion and she had young kids. If she had confessed, she might have gotten leniency. But she wasn't capable of that."

"What happened?" Gayle asked.

"She attacked me with a knife. Unlike her first crime, that was premeditated. What could have been a ten-year sentence ended up being life. I know it was hard. But being honest could cut years off your sentence."

"I don't even care about that. I just want Milton to suffer," she seethed.

"You may feel differently in a few months," Jessie said. In the distance, she thought she could hear the sirens she'd been dreading. Now she found the sound reassuring.

"What are you doing, Milton?" Gayle shouted suddenly.

Jessie spun around on the couch to see Milton Jerebko stomping into the room with a golf club in his hands. He was holding it like a bat.

"You think you can ruin me?" he yelled, his eyes wide and frenzied. "I'm going to *end* you!"

Jessie popped up, blocking his path to his wife, who screamed loudly.

"You don't want to do this, Milton," Jessie said forcefully, putting her hands up like a human stop sign. "You've been a jerk. But you haven't committed a crime yet. If you put the club down, we can still come back from this. But if you don't drop it now, I can't help you."

"You don't give a crap about me," he spat. "All you care about is solving your case. You're like any other hunter who loves the chase. You stalked your prey. Now that you've bagged it, you don't care about the consequences. You don't care about the lives that will be destroyed."

Somewhere in the dark recesses of Jessie's mind, his words struck a chord. But she set them aside. Now wasn't the time for personal introspection.

"You're life hasn't been destroyed yet, Milton," she reminded him. "I know it seems that way. But you can come back from this. It will take time but it can be done. But not if you keep gripping that weapon. You hear those sirens getting louder? What do you think is going to happen when the police burst through the door and see you like that? They're going to shoot you, Milton. Your kids' mother is already going to prison. That's hard enough. Do you want them to have to visit their father in a hole in the ground? For once in your life, think of someone other than yourself. Do the right thing for them. Drop the goddamn club."

The sirens were right outside now. Jessie felt confident that if Jerebko made an aggressive move, she could incapacitate him. He looked strong for his age but he didn't carry himself like someone who was used to being in this kind of situation.

Still, her concern that this go south was real. Murph had almost certainly told the West Hollywood PD that her safety was paramount. If they saw a golf-club-wielding man feet from her, they could easily shoot first and ask questions later.

Milton Jerebko looked genuinely lost. His eyes seemed uncertain but his fingers still gripped the club tightly.

"There's not much time," Jessie implored him. "Drop it."

From behind her, Gayle spoke.

"Milt, drop the club. Hate me all you want. But don't punish our children. They need you. Put it down."

There was a sudden pounding on the door.

"Police—open the door!"

"Milton," Jessie said firmly. "You have about ten seconds to drop the club and get on your knees with your hands up. Otherwise those officers will shoot you. I guarantee it."

"Milt, please!" Gayle begged.

"Open this door now or we will break it down!" came the shout from the front door.

Jerebko seemed to come out of the crazed state he'd been in. He looked down at his hands and then back at Jessie and Gayle.

"Now," Jessie ordered.

Milton dropped the club.

"Good," she said. "Now get on your knees with your hands above your head."

He did as he was told just as the front door was smashed open by a battering ram, which echoed through the house.

"You too, Gayle," Jessie instructed. "Hurry."

Gayle slid to her knees.

Jessie nodded her approval, then yelled as loud as she could.

"We're in here. Suspects are giving up. They are unarmed!"

Then she faced the living room entrance and raised her own hands above her head as a precaution. Seconds later, four uniformed officers burst into the room, all with weapons raised.

"I'm LAPD forensic profiler Jessie Hunt," she announced to them all. "Both suspects on their knees are turning themselves in. Neither is armed."

"Identification!" the officer closest to her demanded.

"Getting it now," she said, slowly moving her right hand to her back pocket.

She had just pulled out her wallet and was preparing to show her ID when Murph walked in with Toomey right behind him. His gun wasn't out but his hand was resting on his holster. A moment later, Dolan walked in behind them.

"That won't be necessary," Murph said emotionlessly. "She is who she says she is. Care to fill us in, Ms. Hunt?"

"Sure," she said, pretending not to be surprised at the lack of anger in his voice. "This is Gayle Martindale Jerebko. She's just confessed to the murder of Claire Stanton. That's Milton Jerebko. He is guilty of…being an asshole. Will we be charging him with anything else today, Gayle?"

Gayle looked at her and then at Milton, who appeared to be crying silently to himself.

"No," Gayle said slowly. "No, we won't."

Jessie nodded as she walked over and kicked the golf club out of Milton's reach.

"Okay then," she said. "I think you can take her into custody. She'll be going to Central Station. Mr. Jerebko, you'll need to travel to the station separately."

"Ms. Hunt, may I have a word with you?" Murph said, his tone professional to anyone who wasn't listening too closely. But she noticed the edge in it.

"Sure," she said, following him into the kitchen. Toomey and Dolan trailed behind.

"I'm glad to see you're okay," Murph said when the four of them were alone in the room. "But as you can imagine, I'm a little disappointed in your lack of communication with the Service prior to your departure."

Jessie looked at him, unsure what to make of his reaction. She thought for certain he'd be screaming at her by now.

"I'm sorry?" she asked more than said.

Dolan chuckled at her confusion.

"He was not this calm on the way over," he said, speaking for the first time since his arrival. "I didn't even know marshals were allowed to talk the way he did."

Murph glared at him but said nothing.

"Listen," Jessie said, knowing some kind of explanation was in order. "I know I shouldn't have just left. But once I realized Gayle was our killer, I saw a way to get her come clean. But I knew she'd never do it if I had all of you around. I had to appeal to her sense of being wronged, of being ignored. I never could have gotten her to that place with all of you in the room."

"We could have waited outside," Dolan said unconvincingly.

Jessie raised her eyebrows.

"Right," she said dismissively, "like you would have agreed to sit out an interview with a murder suspect because I asked politely.

And there is no way the marshal over there would have consented to wait elsewhere while I questioned a person who had just stabbed someone in the throat with keys."

"From what I could tell," Murph said quietly, "it looked like you could have used a bit of backup with Mr. Jerebko. I'm assuming he wasn't working on his stance with that driver at his feet."

"I had it under control," Jessie replied, not wanting to say too much about that particular moment.

"Obviously," he said.

Jessie genuinely couldn't tell if he was sincere or not.

"So are we cool?" she asked.

"That's not how I would describe it," Murph said slowly. "But if you can promise me that you won't ever do something like that again, we can move past it. There are still two serial killers out there looking for you."

She nodded without a word, deciding now wasn't the ideal time to mention that Bolton Crutchfield had been waiting for her at the house.

The officers were escorting Gayle out of the house and into the back of a black-and-white. Jessie and the others followed. Out front, she saw the unmarked vehicle she'd used to get here.

"Don't sweat that," Dolan said, reading her mind. "Decker's sending someone to pick up the car. There's no way he's letting you drive yourself back. You're back to sharing the backseat in the marshal car with me."

They all walked over to get in. As she opened the door, Jessie glanced back in the direction where she'd seen Crutchfield earlier. The last vestiges of dusky light were almost gone and the tree he'd been standing next to was barely visible.

Some of the leafy branches blew gently in the evening breeze and for a second she thought she saw movement from something else, something human. But it was only a shadow caused by a cloud moving through the moonlight.

Is this my life now—jumping at every shifting shadow I see?

She feared that it just might be.

CHAPTER TWENTY FIVE

"I'm sorry."

Jessie turned to Dolan, not certain that she'd really heard the words come out of his mouth.

"Excuse me?" she said, staring at him. "Sorry for what?"

"For what I said before, about you being like your dad. I didn't mean it."

"I didn't think you even remembered saying it, Double Bourbon," she said, trying to keep it light.

"I don't get drunk as fast as I used to," he said. "So my head was still pretty clear at that point."

"Don't worry about it," she said, then after a long moment, added, "Have you talked to anyone about what happened, to your family, I mean?"

"I've talked to lots of people, Hunt. It was Bureau-mandated. I've been through more therapists than pairs of shoes in the last few years."

"Of course," she said. "And I don't mean to butt my head in where it doesn't belong. But I think I've got some expertise in this area. As someone who was strapped down to a chair and forced to watch my mother murdered by my father when I was six, who had to assume a new identity as a child, whose husband tried to kill me and whose adoptive parents were also butchered by my birth father, I think I'm qualified to say this, You need help, man. You are drowning in cynicism. And no amount of bourbon is going to wipe that away."

She waited for him to tell her to mind her business. But he didn't.

"What do you suggest?" he asked, uncharacteristically quiet.

"I see someone semi-regularly who really helps me. Her name is Dr. Janice Lemmon. She's not just a shrink. She's a behavioral therapy specialist. And she used to work as a consultant for the LAPD, among others. She knows her stuff and she doesn't take any crap. I'm about forty percent less messed up than I would be if I didn't see her. I could give you her number."

"Let me think about it," he said.

"I'm giving you the number. You can call her or not. But at least you have it if you need it."

"Thanks, Hunt. You're not as terrible as I thought you'd be."

"Wish I could say the same," Jessie said, smiling.

*

Despite her best efforts, Jessie couldn't stop hearing the words.

"You're like any other hunter who loves the chase," Milton Jerebko had told her. *"You stalked your prey. Now that you've bagged it, you don't care about the consequences. You don't care about the lives that will be destroyed."*

And though Agent Dolan had tried to retract what he'd said about her similarity to her father, the memory of his comments lingered too.

"You both use stealthy techniques to achieve your goals until you determine that a full-on frontal assault is more effective. And you both have terrible impulse control."

There was no point in denying it anymore. Jessie could see the truth now. They were both right. She had inherited her father's relentless love of the hunt. She would use whatever method, no matter how deceptive or morally dubious, to achieve the outcome she wanted.

It mattered that she used that instinct for good and not evil. It mattered a lot. But the impulse to go for the jugular, no matter the consequences, wasn't something she seemed capable of turning off. Truthfully, she didn't really want to.

How much of a push would it require for that impulse to be turned in a darker direction? How much self-control would she have if put in a situation more ambiguous than simply catching the bad guy? What if she turned her ruthlessness against those who had wronged her and not just the system? She couldn't deny that she'd had the urge. Until now, she managed to keep it in check by adhering to a strict personal code. But personal codes can change when put to the test. Could she be sure hers wouldn't?

They were just pulling into the station when the text came through, pulling her out of her reverie. Jessie and Dolan got it at the same time. It was from Decker.

Body found outside Hernandez's hospital. Early indications suggest Xander Thurman. ME confirming.

Jessie gasped involuntarily before reminding herself not to jump to conclusions.

"What is it?" Murph asked from the front seat, sensing there was news.

"They think they found my father," she said evenly.

"Where?"

"The hospital," she said. "I need you to take me there."

Murph shook his head.

"Not until we know it's legit. This could be another trick."

"It could be. That's why I need to go. If anyone can identify the body, it's me. Besides, I'll have you and your buddies there with me. Are you telling me that even with all your resources, you can't protect me in an inherently secure facility like a hospital?"

"I can't be sure it's secure," he countered.

"We'll know it's secure if I can identify the body," Jessie pressed.

Murph didn't respond. From the driver's seat, Toomey looked over. They were almost to the entrance to the police station garage. He clearly wasn't sure if they would be going in.

"You guys go ahead," Dolan volunteered. "I can talk to Gayle Jerebko and get the formal confession from her. I'll call if I have any issues."

Murph continued to stare into the distance for a little longer, then gave Toomey an almost imperceptible nod. As they pulled over to the curb in front of the station, he spoke into his comm.

"Change of plans. Next stop is California Hospital Medical Center. XT may be down. Protectee will attempt to identify. Trail vehicle, stay alert."

Dolan was about to get out of the car, when Jessie tapped him on the shoulder as she reached into her pocket.

"What's this?" he asked, looking at the small recording device in her hand.

"It's Gayle Jerebko's confession. I had to leave my phone in the conference room so I needed something else in case she spilled her

138

guts. Maybe listen to it before you talk to her, so she doesn't try to play you."

"Does she know you recorded this?" Dolan asked.

"Not yet," Jessie said. "I wanted to give her a chance to come clean without being forced into it. But if she starts to get second thoughts, maybe bust this out for her."

Dolan grinned like a kid opening his presents on Christmas morning.

"You are full of surprises, aren't you?" he said.

She didn't respond. But as the car pulled away, she allowed herself a little smile.

CHAPTER TWENTY SIX

The trail team took the lead.

As Toomey circled the block, Collica and Emerson parked and secured the hospital, coordinating with police already on the scene before giving the go-ahead for the other car to park. They pulled onto the staff level of the garage and quickly made their way to the stairs. This time, Toomey stayed right behind Jessie while Murph took the lead.

Once on the main level, an officer led them to a taped off section of the hospital courtyard. Lying under a sheet on the sidewalk close to a flower bed was what Jessie assumed was a body. Blood radiated out from it in every direction. There were other, smaller sheets spread out nearby. Blood also oozed out from under them.

"That him?" Murph asked the officer.

"CSU thinks so," the young man replied.

"Thinks?" Jessie asked.

"It's a little hard to tell," the slightly green-faced officer said. "He's kind of…chopped up."

"What?" Jessie said.

"You should talk to CSU," he said. "They can explain it better."

The three of them walked over to a CSU investigator Jessie recognized.

"What happened, Taylor?" she asked the petite African-American woman, skipping the introductory chit-chat. "I'm hearing making an ID is proving challenging."

"You could say that," she said as she pointed to the upper floors of the building. "It looks like the guy was trying to access the hospital interior through the cooling system. He was on the roof and ran a rope down to a cooling vent on the seventeenth floor. But then things went sideways."

"What does that mean?" Murph asked.

"There's a big circulating fan just a few feet into the duct. It looked like he jammed it with some kind of stopper to prevent the blades from spinning. But something must have gone wrong. It

140

looks like he was just sliding past the fan when the stopper came loose. He got sliced to pieces and shot back out through the vent. That's why there are these…chunks."

Jessie stared at the sheets littering the courtyard. There were eight in total that she could see. Was that how many pieces her father had been chopped into?

She stared at them, waiting for the inevitable emotional response one would expect when seeing a dead parent lying on the ground in lumps of flesh. But there was nothing—certainly not sadness. Not even relief.

"How do you know it's Thurman if he was all chopped up?" Murph asked.

"We found an ID on him. It was for one of his aliases."

"That's it?" Jessie said incredulously. "You're basing an identification on some fake driver's license?"

"Of course not," Taylor said, trying to keep her annoyance in check because of who was asking. "I didn't want to get too detailed. But if you really want to know, we found a couple of fingers on the ground and matched the prints. It was him."

"What about his face?" Murph asked. "Did you try facial recognition on it?"

"We found footage from the surveillance cameras on the roof. They show a man going down the rope. We got a clear shot as he descended. The software called it a ninety-eight percent match for Thurman. It would be even higher but all our images of him are old."

"Did you run it on the dead man?" Murph asked, nodding in the direction of the body parts.

"We tried but it wouldn't give a result. There wasn't much face left to recognize," Taylor said, then added to Jessie "Sorry."

"You don't have to be sensitive with me. I don't care about him," Jessie assured her, increasingly certain that was true. "But I need to see. Maybe I'll be able to identify a feature the system couldn't."

"Ms. Hunt," Taylor said hesitantly. "I'm serious when I say there aren't many features left to identify."

Jessie stared at her coldly for several seconds before responding.

"When he tied me to a chair, strapped my head in place so it couldn't move, and cut into my flesh, I had no choice but to study his features for long stretches. If there's anything left of him, I'll recognize it."

Taylor lowered her head, unable to make eye contact. Then she led Jessie her over to the sheet that covered what appeared to be a head and not much more. She pulled back the sheet to reveal a pulpy mass that was barely discernible as human.

The CSU investigator had been right. There wasn't enough face left to identify what remained as her father. Only the short hair, crushed Adam's apple, and five o'clock shadow smeared in blood offered evidence that it was male.

"Sorry, Taylor," Jessie muttered. "I should have given you the benefit of the doubt."

"That's okay. I get it. Sometimes you just have to see for yourself to be sure."

"How long before the DNA analysis will be in? I want final confirmation on this as soon as possible."

"We're testing the blood now and we'll have preliminary data in a couple of hours," Taylor said. "As you can imagine, there's a rush on this, so we should have a final report by this time tomorrow."

"Can you please ask your supervisor to text me when both versions are done?"

"Of course."

A raindrop landed on Jessie's forearm and she looked up. The moon was no longer visible as a mass of low-hanging clouds hovered overhead.

"Better finish processing the scene quickly," she noted. "It looks like we're going to have more than just sprinkles in a few minutes."

"On it," Taylor said.

Jessie turned to Murph, who looked skeptical.

"Still don't buy it?" she asked.

"It's not that," he said. "This is pretty compelling. But it's my job to be unconvinced until I'm convinced."

"You are preaching to the choir," she said. "I know this man better than just about anyone. He's got more lives than a cat. So I'm not inclined to accept this completely until I get official verification. If I had my way, they'd stitch the chunks back together so I could get confirmation that way."

"I wouldn't hold my breath on that," Murph said, in what Jessie interpreted as an attempt at humor.

"Maybe not," she agreed, smiling grimly. "I guess when your whole life is spent worrying that the boogeyman is going to get you, it's kind of hard to accept that he's no longer a threat. It's almost as if that's his final, sick way of messing with me—making me doubt he's gone even when he's in little pieces."

"Burn him," Toomey said.

"What?' Jessie asked, equally surprised that the guy was speaking and by what he said.

"Have him cremated. Watch his bones burn. It's what they did with plague victims in the Middle Ages to remove all trace of the infection. Burn out the psychological infection by watching him turn to ash."

"Wow, Toomey," she marveled. "You are a seriously dark guy."

"You should hang out with him around Halloween," Murph deadpanned. "He's a blast."

"I'll bet."

"One good thing," Murph noted. "If this turns out to be legit, we're down to one guy hunting you. That's a fifty percent reduction in serial killer threats."

"You're really going for the 'glass half full' take, aren't you?" Jessie said.

"I take my wins where I can get them."

"Fair enough," she said, then transitioned awkwardly to the other issue foremost in her mind. "As long as we're here, you mind if I visit Hernandez? I haven't had a chance to check in on him since the whole stabbing thing."

Murph looked briefly like he might balk, then seemed to change his mind.

"I'll have Collica and Emerson clear the floor. Then we can head up."

As he spoke into his comm, Jessie looked back at the carcass-strewn courtyard. Part of her felt guilty that the sight filled her with no sense of loss.

But only a small part.

*

"Who are you?"

From his hospital bed, Detective Ryan Hernandez was feigning a look of confusion.

143

"Very funny," Jessie said as she entered the room. Murph and Toomey had graciously agreed to wait outside.

"I mean, you kind of look like a gal I partnered with from time to time," he continued, keeping an impressively straight face. "But I haven't seen her in like, forever, so you can't be her."

Jessie didn't reply, waiting to see if she would have to put up with more ribbing. She deserved it. Even if visiting him had been a risk, the remorse she felt at not doing it ate at her.

She looked him over. He still had the same close-cropped dark hair and warm brown eyes she knew so well. But his face was covered in stubble, which she almost never saw. And in the hospital gown, even his well-muscled six-foot, two-hundred-pound frame looked frail. His skin was unusually sallow and he looked worn out.

"I can't believe you let an old man get the upper hand on you," she said, deciding that expressing sincere, genuine concern was not something she was up for in that moment.

"From what I hear, I could probably take him now," Hernandez replied, before sensing that the comment might be out of bounds. "I mean, um, what I mean is…you know what? I'm on a lot of medication right now so you'll have to give me a pass."

"Pass granted," she said, walking over and taking a seat beside him. His joke had broken the dam of reserve inside her and she decided not to hide her concern. "How are you doing, Ryan—for real?"

Hernandez appeared about to make another quip, then stopped himself.

"You really want to hear this?" he asked.

Jessie nodded.

"Okay—not the best," he admitted. "Even with the meds, it hurts every time I, you know, breathe. My arm feels like it's on fire all the time. And I can't seem to sleep for more than two hours at a time. So that kind of sucks. But at least my personal life is falling apart."

"How's that?" Jessie asked, reticent to get specific.

"Well, Shelly hasn't stopped by. I guess if you're separated and your wife doesn't visit you in the hospital after you've been stabbed, it's time to put a nail in that coffin and make it official. I will shortly be a divorced thirty-year-old—just what I always wanted."

"I'm really sorry, Ryan."

"That's okay," he said unconvincingly. "I thought my luck had changed briefly when a nice-looking woman came into the room for a while. But it turned out she was just your body double, here to draw out your dad. Once they found him, even she bailed on me."

"Too bad," Jessie said. "She might have been 'the one.'"

"I've got a couple of months of physical therapy to take my mind off it."

"Way to stay positive there, young fella," she said, deciding it was time to short-circuit the pity party. "Once you're up and moving, I have this great dating website to introduce you to. It brings together hot chicks with wealthy, powerful men...oh, wait, never mind. That doesn't really apply to you, does it?"

He started to laugh, which quickly turned into a groan of pain. When he finally recovered, his spoke more slowly than before.

"I heard through the grapevine that it doesn't just pair the girls up with rich men. Powerful ladies partake as well."

"Yeah," she said, "but the success rate on that is decidedly lower. I don't think they'll be advertising that side of the business anytime soon."

"Seriously, Jessie. Congratulations. Solving a murder case while being protected by US marshals because you're in hiding from two serial killers? That's real gold star material."

"Thank you," she said, unable to come up with anything clever in response.

Ryan picked up the slack.

"And I hear that in the process, you saved the career of a mediocre actor who almost certainly would not have fared well if incarcerated."

"He's actually not that bad an actor," Jessie said. "After having met him, I have to say that projecting on-screen charm really is proof of his talent. Because in real life—not so much with the charm."

"So does that mean you're a big fan of *Bridegroom*?" he teased.

"I'm more passionate about the sequel," she said, unable to suppress a smile. "You know, he's working on a new movie now called *I.T. Guy*. He thinks it may get him award nominations."

There was a long pause in which it looked like Ryan was about to ask her something. But before he did, there was a knock on the door. It was Murph.

"Sorry to interrupt," he said. "But Agent Dolan sent an officer over with your phone and a request to call him when you get a chance."

"Is everything okay?" Jessie asked.

"No idea. That was the entirety of the message."

"Okay, thanks. I'll be right out," she said, then turned back to Ryan. "I guess this is bye for now. But I'll check back in on you tomorrow."

"You sure your bodyguard out there will let you come back?'

"Wild horses couldn't keep me away," she said with a wink.

Then she was out the door and walking away before he could see her face turn a bright shade of crimson.

CHAPTER TWENTY SEVEN

"She copped to all of it."

Jessie listened to her phone on speaker as Dolan gave her the rundown on Gayle Jerebko's confession.

"You didn't have to use the recording?" she asked.

"Nope. She even handed over the keys she used."

"Did she have a lawyer with her?"

"I had barely Mirandized her before she was telling me everything. She gave all the details. The only thing she kept asking was if being honest would get her out in time to see her kids get married."

"Is one of her kids about to get married?" Jessie asked in surprise.

"Eventually, I guess," Dolan said. "But right now, they're teenagers. I told her I couldn't promise anything but that I'd bring it up with the prosecutor."

"You don't sound committed to doing that," Jessie noted.

"It might be better if you make the case, Hunt."

"Why?"

"Because I'm not sure how convincing I'd be. She killed a girl by jamming keys in her throat. I don't care if she has kids. That demands justice."

Jessie didn't disagree, though the fact that she'd used the possibility of leniency as a means of getting the confession gave her a bit of pause. Dolan apparently didn't expect an answer because he barreled onto another topic.

"Anyway, enough about that. We caught the killer."

"I caught the killer," Jessie corrected.

"Whatever," he continued, undeterred. "The killer's been caught. Your father won't be dropping in anytime soon. And based on the lifesaving tip he gave you at the bar last night before knocking you out, Crutchfield seems more interested in being your bestie than doing you harm. I'd say all of that calls for a drink or five. What say we meet up later? You can even bring that surly bastard Murphy along if you want."

"You're on speaker, Dolan. And Murph is in the room with me."

"I knew that," Dolan said unpersuasively after a brief pause. "You don't think I knew that?"

"Hello, Agent," Murph said, apparently untroubled by the dig.

"Hello, Marshal," Dolan replied. "You in?"

"Agent Dolan," Murph said, "despite your confidence that Bolton Crutchfield is harmless and that Xander Thurman is dead, I'm not entirely certain of either of those things. Until I am, I think it would be inadvisable to go on a bender."

"I get where you're coming from, Marshal. But I think a celebratory toast isn't going to do any harm. You all can go back to wherever that safe house is afterward and I'll stick around. We can go to the same bar as before. Only this time you can have people encircle the whole place, maybe even stand on manhole covers. You can search everyone who walks in. Considering they'd all be cops, I doubt there would be a problem. What do you say?"

Jessie looked over at the marshal. Whether it was the long day, the solved case, or her dead father, he looked tempted. He seemed about to cave for a moment. But then his face hardened and Jessie knew it wasn't going to happen.

"It's not looking good," she said into the phone. "He's got that humorless look, Dolan."

"I'm sorry, Agent," Murph said, verifying her suspicions. "We've had enough close calls for one day. Perhaps another time."

There was such a long silence on the other end of the line that Jessie thought he might have hung up.

"You, Murphy," Dolan finally said, "are what the experts call a bummer. And for that reason, I will not have a drink in honor. No sir!"

"I'll have to find a way to muddle through," Murph muttered.

"However," Dolan continued, either not hearing him or not caring, "I will down one on your behalf, Jessie Hunt. You're good people."

"I'm humbled," she said, not entirely sure he hadn't started already.

"As well you should be," he said.

A second later the line went dead.

"I think you hurt his feelings," Jessie said to Murphy, only half-joking.

"I think you may be right," Murph agreed.

Jessie's phone pinged.

"Maybe he's trying again," she said as she opened the text.

The words on the screen sent a wave of adrenaline coursing through her body.

"Is it him?" Murph asked.

"No. It's the CSU supervisor. They verified the DNA in the blood samples from the hospital courtyard. It's my father's."

*

Jessie couldn't control the thoughts swimming in her head.

Sitting in the backseat of the Marshal Service car, with Toomey and Murph, she barely saw the buildings passing by. The sprinkles from the hospital courtyard had turned into full on rain. But she barely acknowledged it as it battered the sedan roof.

Her father was actually dead. Somehow she'd been certain that if he ever died, it would be at her hands. She'd counted on it, in fact. As a result, mixed in with the relief she now finally allowed herself to feel at his death was the strange sense that she still had unfinished business.

It was as if he'd somehow robbed her of the catharsis she'd been hoping for by dying in such an ignominious fashion. The irony didn't escape her: it wasn't until she learned she'd never get vengeance that Jessie realized how much she'd been after it all along.

"Okay," Murph said, breaking into her trance, "you can text Dolan. Tell him we'll meet for one toast and then we're out of there."

It took Jessie a moment to process what he'd said.

"Why are you changing your mind?" she asked.

"Thurman's death makes it an easier call. I think we can protect you short term at the bar if we're only watching out for one threat. And honestly, you really look like you need a drink."

Jessie thought about it for a second and then decided she was sick of thinking for a while.

149

"I am going to defer to your judgment on this one," she said, getting out her phone and texting Dolan to meet them at Bob's Frolic Four forthwith.

As she waited for a reply, she listened to Murph give the revised plan to the trail unit over the comm. He was also requesting LAPD backup to the scene.

"All this so little ol' me can get a drink?" she asked when he was done.

"All this so I don't lose my job for getting little ol' you a drink," he corrected.

The bar was close but with the traffic and rain-soaked streets, it took a good ten minutes to get there. When they arrived, there were already multiple cars double parked in front. The place was a madhouse.

"Maybe we should park in the residential section," Jessie suggested. "It might be less crowded and it's only a few blocks of walking."

"Can't do it," he replied. "Walking any distance while exposed is too risky. We need to be able to access the car quickly if necessary. Also, I don't want to get wet."

Jessie couldn't argue the last point. Murph spoke into his comm.

"Trail team, we're going to circle while you get things squared away. Once you've parked, Collica—take the front of the bar. Emerson, take the back. You can let us in through the alley entrance. Toomey will circle the location while we're inside."

While they circled, waiting for the trail team to get set up, Jessie texted Dolan again to let him know they were about to go in. His reply was succinct.

There in ten. Order me a bourbon—double.

"Okay, team, we are on the move," Murph said, getting her attention. "Toomey, drop us close to the alley door and resume circling. Emerson, prepare to open the back door. Collica, take up position at the entrance to the back room. Get ID on anyone who wants to enter. Pull rank if someone gives you static. You ready, Hunt?"

"I've never had so much effort put into getting me a drink, not even on dates."

"Are you ready?" he repeated not playing along.

"Ready," she said, matching his straight face. Murph nodded back.

"We are a go," he said, getting out and opening the back door for her. "Toomey—resume circling the block. Emerson, open that door now."

Toomey waited until he saw the bar's back door open before driving off down the alley toward the main street again. Emerson held the door open as Jessie and Murph jogged toward it, trying not to get soaked while also avoiding slipping on the slick asphalt.

Emerson gave them a goofy half smile that suggested he was glad to be dry. He was a big dude, easily six foot two, with a military-style buzz cut that made it hard to even be sure his hair was blond. But in that moment, with the silly grin on his face, he looked less like a hardened law enforcement professional and more like a pre-teen boy who was giddy at his good fortune.

A loud bang suddenly echoed through the alley. Emerson's face froze. A fraction of a second later, blood began pouring from a small hole in his forehead. The smile was still on his lips as he fell backward into the bar. The door he was holding open slammed shut.

Jessie stared at the spot where he used to be in stunned silence. A sudden rush of panicked nausea rose up in her throat and she felt sure she would vomit. She wanted to bend over but her knees seemed frozen in place.

"Get down!" Murph shouted, shoving her toward the ground.

On her knees now, Jessie embraced the cold puddle quickly soaking her pants. Using the rush of bracingly cold water to snap herself back into the moment, she spun around, looking for the source of the shot. Before she could discern anything, Murph was in front of her, using his body to block any future shots. His gun was pointed back down the alley. Jessie turned back to the bar door and tried to open it, without success.

"It's locked," she said.

Murph spoke into his comm, his voice surprisingly calm.

"Shot fired. Man down. Repeat—Emerson is down. We are in the alley. The back door to the club is locked. Requesting assistance." Then, still looking back in the direction of the shot, he addressed her. "Let's go around front. Stay ahead of me. All units, we are using the side alley to return to the front of the bar. Meet us there."

"I'm around the east side of the club in the other alley," Toomey said urgently. "It's going to take a minute to get there."

"Approaching the back door now," Collica added.

"Do not exit through the back, Collica," Murph ordered. "The shooter has eyes on that door. Return to the front."

As the two of them ran, there was a screeching sound behind them. Jessie looked back over her shoulder. A compact car with its headlights off was tearing down the alley toward them. With the rain and darkness, she couldn't identify the driver.

Whoever it was barreled straight for them. It was clear that they wouldn't get out of the alley to the sidewalk before they were mowed down. Jessie's eyes darted left and right, looking for any doorway or nook to take shelter in. She saw Murph doing the same thing.

Steps ahead of her, he came to a door with a padlock on it and fired once, shattering the thing. Then he yanked the door open, grabbed her, and literally tossed her through the entryway. As she fell to the ground, she looked back to the alley just in time to see him take one step toward her.

Then he disappeared from her sight, hit by the hood of the car. She heard the thud of the vehicle against his body and then another one seconds later when he landed. It was quieter than she expected, as if he'd traveled a great distance.

The car tires squealed as it braked hard. She saw the taillights illuminate as it backed up until she could see the front passenger seat. The automatic window rolled down and the driver looked over at her with a wolfish grin on his face.

"Hi, Junebug," her father said.

CHAPTER TWENTY EIGHT

For the briefest of moments, Jessie thought she was dreaming.

She'd had so many nightmares in which her father appeared out of nowhere to harm people helping her that she wasn't entirely sure it was real this time.

It was only when he got out of the car and slammed the door shut that her brain snapped back into reality. The alley was real. The rain was real. The car that had just hit Murph was real. And her father, the serial killer she'd been assured was dead only minutes earlier, was real too.

He looked much as he had the last time she'd seen him, when he ambushed her in her apartment only weeks ago. He still had the lean, lanky body, though he appeared more hunched over than before. His dark hair, dotted with visible gray even in the half light of the alley, was longer than before. But his green eyes, the same shade as hers, had lost none of their maniacal gleam.

Ignoring the pain in her hip where she'd landed on the floor, she scrambled to her feet, reaching for the small pistol in her ankle holster. Her adrenaline was pumping so hard her fingers shook slightly.

Even as they settled down, she had trouble freeing the gun and looked down to see what the issue was. The holster was snagged on the cuff of her pants. She ripped the cuff and yanked out the gun, pointing it back at the alley. Her father was gone.

She backed away, her weapon pointed at the car. She could feel herself hyperventilating and mentally shouted an order to slow her breathing. It would help her get a more accurate shot and, equally important, not pass out. As she exhaled, a voice called out.

"Your marshal buddy doesn't look too good, Junebug. One of his legs is bent the wrong way. It's kind of gross. I think I'm going to put him out of his misery. I'll be right back."

She heard footsteps move in Murph's direction and shouted out to the emptiness.

153

"If you go for him, I'll get away. By the time you come back for me, I'll be long gone. So you can try to take out some random guy who doesn't matter to you. Or you can come for me. But you can't do both."

She heard the footsteps stop. While he decided, she looked behind her to see if she really could get away. What she found filled her with disquiet. For a moment she thought she was being stared at by dozens of motionless figures.

After a second she realized that she was in some kind of warehouse, filled with what appeared to be hundreds of department store mannequins. Some were completed while others lay on the ground half-finished or abandoned. She scurried back into the depths so that she wouldn't be an easy target if he appeared at that moment.

"I guess this is goodbye," she yelled behind her, hoping to force her father's hand.

"You drive a hard bargain," she heard him say, obviously getting closer. "Considering that your marshal buddy's friends will likely be here any minute, you've won me over. I'm coming for you, little girl."

She was tempted to hide behind a mannequin and take a shot when he came into view. But then she pushed the idea out of her head. He had a gun too. A fair fight wasn't to her advantage. The smart move was to find a way out of here, get back to the bar, and call in the cavalry.

She looked around, desperately searching for an "exit" sign. She saw one illuminated in green at the far end of the warehouse and moved in that direction. Glancing back, she saw that her father still wasn't visible in the doorway.

"Last chance," she shouted so as to be heard over the rain. "Better come now or all that hard work will be for nothing, Xander."

She had barely finished speaking when the shots began. He fired three times as he moved into the warehouse. She hurried further back toward the exit, darting among the mannequins so that he wouldn't have an easy shot if he located her.

"You know, Junebug," he called out, "it's disrespectful to refer to your parent by his first name. I'll accept Daddy, Father, or my personal preference, Pa. But Xander? That's just rude. I thought I raised you better than that."

Jessie tried to move as quietly as possible as she navigated her way to the exit. The sound of his voice and footsteps was actually reassuring. At least she knew he wasn't focused on Murph any longer. Besides, she'd rather have him taunt her if it meant she knew where he was.

She was only steps from the exit when her phone rang. For a second her whole body went stiff. Then, as quickly as she could, she slid behind a large mannequin, pulled it out of her pocket, and silenced it. The caller ID showed that it was Dolan, who was probably still unaware of everything going on.

"You were so close to getting out," Xander called out, his footsteps moving rapidly in her direction. "But now I know where you are. The light from that exit sign should frame you nicely when I shoot you as you try to leave."

Jessie glanced around, looking for another way out. But none was visible. He was right. If she tried to make a run for it, he'd have a clear shot at her. Based on what he'd just done to Emerson, she didn't want to give him the chance.

She guessed she had about twenty seconds until he was to her. The one thing working for her was that when he got there, she'd be surrounded by thirty to forty mannequins who could easily be mistaken for her. She decided to make it more challenging.

Placing the pistol delicately on a cardboard box, she pulled off her jacket to reveal the cream-colored top she was wearing. It wasn't as white as the mannequins. But it would help her blend in a bit.

She picked up the pistol and took up a position between two mannequins—one male and one female. The sliver of space between them was just wide enough for her to aim through.

The footsteps stopped and she knew he was close, though she couldn't see him. As she waited, trying to breathe silently, she heard his breaths, loud and wheezy. A thought belatedly registered in her mind.

Xander's footsteps when he was running moments earlier were uneven, almost as if he was half-shuffling one of his legs. That and his labored breathing reminded her of something she'd forgotten in the terror of the situation. He was injured.

It had been only weeks since he'd been shot in the abdomen and shoulder, smashed in the skull with a nightstick, and jumped out of an apartment window. Detective Ryan Hernandez, thirty years old and in great shape, was expected to take two months to recover from two stab wounds. How weak and tired must a fifty-something man feel with vastly worse injuries? The realization filled her with hope and another, far less expected feeling: confidence.

If I can get that gun out of his hand, I'll have the physical advantage. But how?

She looked around and her eyes fell on two unattached mannequin pieces. One was a head and the other was an arm from shoulder to fingertips. She had the kernel of an idea. Under normal circumstances, she'd take a moment to try to anticipate how it might play out. But these weren't normal circumstances and she didn't have time formulate all the details. This would either work or it wouldn't. She was about to find out.

Shoving the gun in her front pocket, she grabbed both mannequin body parts. She tiptoed forward a bit until she could catch of glimpse of Xander. He was spinning back and forth between her direction and the other side of the warehouse, unsure which side she was hiding on.

She was about to toss the mannequin parts when a sudden explosion rocked the warehouse, making the walls shudder and sending some of the mannequins toppling over. After the racket subsided, he shouted to her.

"You're probably wondering what that noise is all about. Don't worry, Junebug. It's just my car exploding. I set a timer on it. That ought to distract your law enforcement buddies for a while. That way we can get some uninterrupted quality time. Sound good?"

He was still swiveling back and forth, trying to catch sight of her. Despite her anxiousness, Jessie tried to remain patient, waiting until the echo from the exploding car had faded and until his attention was elsewhere.

Then she got her chance. When he briefly turned the other way, she tossed the mannequin head in the air, high overhead so that it he couldn't see it. It hit something about twenty feet in front of him before landing on the ground, reverberating loudly in the now otherwise quiet warehouse.

He spun in that direction, pointing but not firing. Jessie skulked forward several steps, then launched the unattached arm at a mannequin closer to her father. It landed with a thud, making the full-sized body careen backward, colliding into multiple other mannequins like human-shaped bowling pins going down all at once.

Using the cacophony of noise as cover, she pulled out the pistol and sprinted toward him. Initially startled, Xander regrouped quickly. He must have sensed the move was a diversion because he quickly spun around, pointing his gun in her general direction.

She fired at him as she ran, aware that with the multiple mannequins between them, she was unlikely to hit him. That wasn't even her primary goal. She was hoping that he would try to duck or dive or even just flinch long enough for her to get within fighting distance of him.

It partly worked. He did flinch, but only briefly. Recovering, it took only a couple of seconds for him to turn his gun on her. No longer concerned with stealth and now less than ten feet away, she slammed toward him, knocking over as many mannequins as possible so as to disorient him. She was only steps away when he locked in on her.

As he pointed his weapon, she shoved the last remaining mannequin torso between them at him with her left hand as she fired wildly with her right. At that moment, the mannequin's chest exploded in front of her, spraying a cloud of dust everywhere.

And then she was on him, colliding hard into his body with every ounce of force she could muster. Her pistol flew out of her hand as she landed on top of him, hearing the air get sucked from his chest. As she rolled over, she saw that his hands were empty and heard his gun slide off somewhere out of view.

Pulling herself to her feet, she advanced on him. He rolled over onto his stomach and pushed up onto all fours just in time for her to kick him square in the chest. He toppled over backward, his now-longish hair falling forward to cover his forehead and part of his eyes. He flailed wildly in the sea of mannequin limbs that lay on the ground all around him

She stepped toward him, anxious to take advantage of his diminished state but still wary that he might have a hidden weapon somewhere. To Xander Thurman, being without a knife was like most people being without clothes. She found it hard to believe he didn't have one.

"Wait. Please," he groaned as she approached. "I only want to talk. That's all I ever wanted."

She hesitated for only a half a second, processing the comment and almost immediately dismissing it. After all, that exploding mannequin he'd shot up moments earlier could have been her. But

157

Thurman took advantage of that half second, swinging at her with the leg of a mannequin she hadn't realized he'd been gripping.

It collided with her left knee and her leg gave out. She dropped to the floor right in front of him as he swung the leg the other way, slamming the heel into her temple. She sprawled onto her side, briefly stunned by the impact.

She heard him clambering to his feet and tried to do the same. But as she stood, her leg wobbled and gave out again, She dropped to her knees and felt a rush of pain as her kneecaps slammed onto the concrete floor. She looked up and saw that Xander was on his feet now, still holding the mannequin leg. He pulled it back behind his head like a baseball bat and took a step toward her.

CHAPTER TWENTY NINE

Jessie Hunt, injured and disoriented, stared at her father as he moved toward her.

Her mind flashed back to another time, many years ago, when she thought she had escaped her father. She was called Jessica Thurman back then. Six years old, she'd been tied to a wooden chair with her eyelids taped open in an isolated, snowbound Ozarks cabin. Her mother stood in front of her, her arms strapped to an overhead wooden beam.

While he made Jessica watch, her father used his hunting knife to gut her mom. Then he left the room, making his daughter sit there, unblinking, as the life slowly drained from her mother's body and she went limp, her arms dangling uselessly above her head.

At some point Jessica had escaped, running out barefoot into the snowy woods. She ran for a long time. Eventually her feet grew numb. But still she ran, trying to stay ahead of the heavy, booted footsteps not far behind.

Finally she came to a cliff's edge and looked over to see a raging river fifty feet below. She knew, even then, that jumping off that cliff would be suicide. But it felt preferable to the alternative.

And yet, when the moment came, when her father's arm reached out to pull her back, she found that she couldn't take the leap, couldn't move at all. So he dragged her back through the snow, re-strapped her to the chair, and left her in that cabin with the body of her mother. Only a couple of hunters passing by three days later saved her from certain death.

There was no forgetting, and there were no hunters here to save her now. As her father got closer, she knew that there was no one left to protect her from the monster who had tortured her in both life and dreams. There was only her.

So she stood up.

Ignoring the pain in her leg, she forced herself to her feet in one swift deliberate motion. When her father reached her, she was upright, her fists clenched, her body taut and ready, her eyes trained on his. He stopped moving forward, his own eyes betraying his uncertainty.

"Come on!" she screamed.

But he didn't. Instead of continuing forward, Xander Thurman tossed the mannequin leg at her, turned, and ran toward the exit, his right leg dragging slightly.

Jessie stood frozen for a moment, not sure what had just happened. Then she stepped forward to chase after him.

She had to stop immediately. Her leg hurt but that wasn't the real problem. She still felt woozy from the blow to her head. She bent over slightly, trying to keep the room from spinning. She watched, frustrated and helpless as her father pushed open the exit door and disappeared from sight.

She allowed herself five seconds to recuperate, taking in several deep breaths, hoping that her head would clear. It helped. She didn't feel totally lucid but she no longer feared that she would topple over if she tried to walk.

She took one step. Her leg held steady. She took another. The knee was sore but she could put weight on it. She took a third step. And then, confident that she could stay upright, she broke into a run, out the door, in search of the father who wanted to kill her.

*

She was getting close now.

After leaving the warehouse, she briefly thought she'd lost him. But then she saw the limping figure about fifty yards ahead of her. He was moving away from the business district and toward the adjacent residential area.

As she ran, Jessie pulled out her phone and auto-dialed Dolan's number, trying not to lose her grip in the downpour. It went straight to voicemail.

"Dolan," she yelled breathlessly into the phone. "I'm chasing Thurman. He hit Murph with a car and chased me into a warehouse. I disarmed him but he got away. He's currently running westbound on West 25th Street into the West Adams residential zone. My ringer is off but you can track my location."

As she tried to shove the phone back in her pocket, her fingers slipped and it fell from her grip. It hit the ground and slid along the asphalt until it ended up in the gutter, where it was carried along by the torrent of water.

Everything after that seemed to happen in slow motion. Jessie watched as the fast-moving current tugged the phone swiftly toward a storm drain. Realizing she couldn't catch up in time, she dove to try to snag it. But as she leapt, her left leg buckled and she landed well short, crushing her ribs and knocking the wind out of herself. She could only lie helplessly in the rain as her phone disappeared from sight.

When she managed to get to her knees and crawl over, she reached her hand in, hoping the phone had lodged against the grate but knowing it hadn't. Finding nothing, she looked up and saw that her father was now a good hundred yards ahead of her, even with his pronounced limp.

The phone doesn't matter. Get up. Get him.

She pushed herself upright, pretending not to notice her throbbing knee or her screaming ribs. As she started to get some momentum again, she saw Xander round the corner north onto 2nd Avenue. She picked up the pace so as not to lose sight of him.

He was still visible when she got to the intersection. She had made up some of the distance, even at her slowed pace. He looked back at her and, seeming to decide that a chase on open streets was ultimately a losing battle for him, ran up the sidewalk toward one of the expansive manor houses on that street.

As Jessie hurried to catch up, she saw him reach the door and grab the knob. She willed it not to open. But it did. He looked back down the street at her, gave a malevolent grin, and stepped inside.

By the time she reached the house almost a minute later, Jessie knew her advantage was gone. Xander could be just inside the door, waiting with a fireplace poker or a butcher knife. But at least he was trapped. Dolan would get her message and in just a few minutes, this street would be swarming with cops. All she had to do was sit and wave them down when they arrived.

Then she heard the scream.

CHAPTER THIRTY

Jessie ran up the steps.

She couldn't wait. That wasn't the scream of someone who was simply scared. It was a person in unrelenting pain. Another scream cut through the night air. And she had to make it stop.

Even as she reached the top of the stairs and saw that the front door was ajar, she knew she was being manipulated, that she was doing exactly what Thurman wanted. And yet she couldn't stop herself. She couldn't just stand on the street and wait for backup. Her father's victim would be dead by then.

But just because she had to enter didn't mean she had to be predictable about it. She dove at the door, extending her arms to push it open, before tucking her head into a roll at the last moment, just as her FBI field instructor had taught her. She somersaulted into the house and used her momentum to pop right up and spin around quickly, looking for any immediate threat. There was no one in the foyer.

Then she heard another scream. It was coming from somewhere in the center of the house. She rushed down the closest hallway, and as she approached the entryway to the large room ahead of her, used the same move to roll into it rather than run in upright.

When she popped up, she whirled around the room to look for threats. What she saw made her mouth drop open. Across the massive living room, in front of a crackling fireplace, was a girl. She was sitting in a chair, her arms strapped to the armrests, her feet bound to the chair's legs. Her eyelids were taped open.

But her mouth was stuffed with a rag. The screams weren't coming from her. Instead, they seemed to be coming from the woman in front of her, whose arms, tied to an overhead roof beam with bungee cord, dangled above her head. Jessie saw that a steady stream of blood was seeping onto the floor from her midsection. Next to her, a man dangled limply, a huge pool of blood at his feet. He looked to be dead.

162

Jessie glanced around for any sign of Thurman. He was almost certainly around, as evidenced by the recent screaming. But he wasn't immediately visible. Though she had no choice but to move forward, something felt off about the situation to Jessie. How had her father prepared this elaborate setup so quickly?

Her eyes fell on the poker to the right of the fireplace. Moving cautiously, she edged toward it, hoping to secure any weapon that could even the odds. As she reached the couch, she peered around it in case he was hiding behind it. There was no sign of him.

She continued toward the fireplace, passing the dangling man and the moaning woman to his left. She wanted to help, but refused to even look over at them. Any distraction might give Thurman, wherever he was, a chance to make a move.

She got around the couch and was within feet of the poker when she allowed a passing glance at the girl seated within reach of her. Closer now, Jessie realized that she wasn't so much a girl as a young woman. She looked to be in her late teens.

Despite her best efforts not to, Jessie looked at the girl's eyes. Taped wide open, they looked terrified. But there was something else in them too. There was intent. She seemed to be trying to convey something to Jessie, who studied her more closely.

The girl's eyes were moving, darting to a spot to Jessie's right and then back to her. Jessie glanced to the right, expecting to see Thurman crouched there. But what she saw instead was a pair of shoes. Just beyond them were the sock-covered feet of someone lying face down on the floor.

Another dead body, just like the man dangling behind her?

And that's when it clicked for her. The girl's eyes weren't bouncing between the body on the floor and Jessie. They were bouncing between the body on the floor and the man dangling behind her.

She turned around to face him, knowing it was already too late. She was right. The man behind her was no longer dangling and his arms were no longer above his head. One of them, the one injured from the gunshot to the shoulder a few ago, rested at his side. But the other one, already swinging a candlestick holder toward her head, worked fine.

The arm moved smoothly and quickly as the candlestick holder connected with the side of her skull, just a millisecond after she recognized the person holding it as her father.

163

CHAPTER THIRTY ONE

Jessie was pretty sure she wasn't dead, though part of her wished she was.

As she slowly returned to consciousness, her body began to throb. It was hard to discern exactly where the pain was coming from, there so many sources of it. As she waited for her vision to unblur, she did a mental rundown of her personal injuries.

Her head throbbed relentlessly where the candlestick holder had smashed into it. Her ribs ached from diving onto the street after her phone. Her hip was sore from landing on it when Murph had thrown her out of the path of the oncoming car. Her knee felt swollen, like a balloon that needed some air let out.

And there were her arms. She hadn't injured them as best she could recall. So why did they sting so bad?

As her eyes slowly cleared, she realized the reason. They were tied to bungee cords and wrapped around the overhead beam, just like the woman next to her, who was now clearly dead.

Jessie quickly closed her eyes, trying not to let the sight linger in her brain. She was still too hazy to be truly scared yet. But she knew that feeling was coming. And being inches from a dead woman in the same position as her wasn't going to help fight that off.

She could hear movement somewhere in front of her and assumed it was Thurman, since everyone else in the room was either dead or tied up. She tried not to move, hoping that the longer she could make him think she was still out, the more time she would have to come up with a plan.

Based on the fact that her arms weren't totally numb but still tingled with pain, she gathered she hadn't been out more than a few minutes. Despite the discomfort, she preferred this. Once her arms became completely numb, they'd be mostly useless—unable to grip anything that might help her escape. She needed to find a way out of this fast, while her body still had some capacity to function and before her father began the inevitable cutting.

"I know you're conscious, Junebug," Thurman said mildly from what sounded like only a few feet away. "Your breathing changed when you woke up."

Since her ruse was now pointless, Jessie allowed herself to swallow. It turned into a hacking cough as her throat was dry. The shaking of her body made every injury hurt exponentially more.

"I don't normally do this," Xander said, his voice getting closer. "But since we're kin, I'm going to give you a little liquid refreshment."

Suddenly her head was being tilted back and water poured down her throat. She almost choked but still managed to gulp a bit down. Her vision grew crisper, enough that she could see the man standing directly in front of her. He smiled.

"Of course, there's a price for every blessing we receive in life," he continued as he pulled out a long butcher knife already caked in blood and swung it casually at her mid-section, slicing into her side. "This is yours."

She gasped at this new unexpected pain. She knew the cut wasn't very deep but that didn't make it hurt any less. It felt like someone was pressing a hot pan against the left side of her stomach. Despite that, she refused to scream. Instead she inhaled deeply and then tried to breathe the agony out with the carbon dioxide.

"I have to say," she muttered when she was sure she could get out a sentence without crying, "I thought our reunion days were over. I was getting all geared up to mourn you."

Jessie waited for his response, hoping desperately that his vanity would at least temporarily take precedence over his thirst for vengeance. If she could get him to talk about how he'd survived what everyone assumed was his death, he might delay whatever awful plan he had in store her.

"You did jump the gun on that one," he said, taking the bait. "I thought if anyone would figure out my little subterfuge, it would be you, Junebug. But, as ever, my own daughter disappoints."

He took another casual swipe with the knife, this time getting her in the right thigh. The material of her pants was thicker than her shirt so the cut didn't go quite as deep. But it still required enormous effort for her to stay quiet and deny him the satisfaction of seeing her suffer.

She tried to focus her attention on something other than his contorted smirk. Looking down, she noticed that his left hand, the one not holding the knife, was bandaged up. Specifically, his middle and pinkie fingers were tightly wrapped in gauze. She nodded at them.

"I guess that explains how they found your fingers at the scene."

He smiled proudly.

"I had to make it believable," he said. "Sometimes that requires a bit of personal sacrifice."

"But it wasn't just the fingers, Xander," she reminded him through gritted teeth. "They found your DNA in the blood in the courtyard. I don't think it was crazy to assume those chunks of flesh were yours."

"Of course it might have looked that way to the untrained eye," he conceded. "But all it took was little creative thinking to uncover the truth."

"Humor me, Pa," she said sarcastically. "You know you want to tell me how you did it. And I'm really the only one who would appreciate it. So you may as well just spit it out."

She glanced over at the teenage girl tied up in the chair across from her, whose expression was one of bewilderment at this crazy woman baiting the man with the knife. Jessie smiled to herself. At least that meant she was doing a solid job of it.

"I'll make you a deal," Thurman said devilishly. "I'll tell you how I did it if you promise to keep it a secret. Oh wait, what am I saying? You'll be keeping *everything* a secret soon enough."

He chuckled quietly at his own joke before continuing.

"So I guess I can share. After all, sharing is caring, right, Junebug?"

"If you say so."

"No," he growled. "I want *you* to say so."

Jessie gulped hard.

"Sharing is caring," she muttered.

"Good job, little one," he said happily. "So here's the great thing about hospitals—they bring in unconscious people. So if you find a homeless person who matches your size, age, and general looks and poison him very near the hospital you want to access later, they'll admit him. Then all you have to do is sneak into the hospital before the big security clampdown, collect the unguarded unconscious man, and take him to a little-used basement storage room where you now have all the time you need to do a total blood exchange, which is a massive transfusion, replacing all his blood with your own. And if you've been accumulating and storing your blood in a refrigerator at that very hospital over several weeks, the entire process is actually very efficient. The machine that does it is mobile and everything. Modern technology is a marvel, Junebug."

"Sounds like a snap," Jessie said sarcastically, knowing her father would appreciate her reluctantly noting just how difficult that process must actually have been.

"If you're prepared, yes," he agreed. "Then all you have to do is put your extra clothes with your fake ID on the unconscious man, take him up to an industrial duct fan near a courtyard-facing vent, and shove him through. He'll come down in pieces like candy dropping from a piñata."

He paused briefly, almost as if he was waiting for applause. When none was forthcoming, he continued.

"And if you set things up ahead of time by shimmying down a rope to that vent when you know you're on a camera that will be checked later, you've doubled your 'confirmation of fake death' pleasure. Chopped up body that looks like me? Check. My fake ID left with the body? Check. Surveillance video of me entering the vent? Check. My actual DNA splattered all over the scene? Checkmate."

"That is pretty clever," Jessie whispered hoarsely. "But how did you find me at the bar?"

As she asked the question, she rocked back and forth as if in terrible discomfort. She was but that wasn't the point. She was trying to keep her arms from losing all sensation. Getting good old dad to describe his exploits was a useful way to extend her life. But if she didn't have any way to prevent him from using that knife, all the delaying tricks would be for naught.

Her father didn't seem troubled by her movement. In fact, seeing the blood from her wounds drip wildly on the floor as if she was the brush for an unfinished Jackson Pollock painting seemed to give him great pleasure.

"That was easy too," he said. "After he escaped, I had a powwow with our mutual acquaintance, Bolton Crutchfield. He helped tidy up a few of the boo-boos I got in our last encounter. But I was suspicious that his loyalties might have been compromised. He used to be such a devoted young man, eager to learn, happy to do my bidding without question. But then he met you and he seemed to go a bit soft. His affection for you clouded his judgment. And when he learned I was going to punish you for good, he seemed…unenthusiastic."

"Traitor," Jessie volunteered sarcastically.

"Indeed," Thurman agreed. "Luckily, I fed him a story about learning the location of your safe house, which was, I admit, a ruse. I also put a tracker with a bug on him. He didn't expect an old fella like myself to use such new-fangled technology. That's how I followed him to the bar. That's how I learned he'd warned you about my possible attack on the safe house. That's how I knew you'd almost certainly go back to that same bar to celebrate my "demise." But in case you're wondering, let me assure you, once I'm done with you, I'll be paying a visit to Mr. Crutchfield to let him know just how I feel about his treachery."

Jessie ignored the Crutchfield threat. His safety was pretty low on her list of priorities. Stalling her father long enough to get full feeling back in her arms was at the top.

She saw the girl trying to take advantage of the delay too. Whenever Thurman looked away from her, she managed to maneuver the rag stuffed in her mouth out just a little bit more. From the cuts on her swollen, discolored lips, Jessie could tell she'd probably been trying to get the thing out of her mouth for hours. She looked like she was close to spitting it out entirely, not that it would do her much good.

"But you couldn't have known when we'd be at the bar," Jessie pointed out, drawing his attention back to her. "How did you have time to tie up the people who live here?"

"The people who live here?' he repeated, amused. "These folks don't live here, Junebug. The owners of this house have been out of town for a week. I brought in these fine citizens from another neighborhood altogether."

Jessie, amid all the blood and madness, found that extra perplexing.

"But why them? These are innocent people."

Xander laughed.

"No one is truly innocent. You should know that by now, Junebug. Besides, it's going to be so much fun watching this girl watch you die. I'll get a front row seat. And despite all your stalling, I'll still have time to leave. Your FBI friend and his lackeys have to go house to house searching for you. By the time they get here, you'll be dead and I'll be long gone."

"Why are you doing this?" Jessie asked, genuinely dumbfounded.

"Oh, wouldn't you like to know," he said gleefully. "I almost want you to live just you so can learn the big twist. I would love to see the look on your face when you discovered the truth. Unfortunately, you are *part* of the twist, so it's just not possible. Isn't it ironic? Anyway, enough chit-chat. It's daughter gutting time."

With that, he stopped talking and advanced on her.

CHAPTER THIRTY TWO

Jessie wasn't ready.

Her arms still felt floppy and weak, like a rag doll. As Xander moved closer, she watched him almost spring with enthusiasm. His once-short hair, now flopping over his forehead, bounced up and down.

As he approached, she noticed something she'd been too frantic to pick up on earlier. Underneath his drooping hair, on the right side of his forehead, was a small flesh-colored bandage.

It occurred to her that it was in the exact same spot that Bolton Crutchfield had circled on his own forehead earlier this evening as he stood by the tree outside the Jerebko house. She doubted it was a coincidence. Was Crutchfield trying to tell her something? If, as Thurman suspected, his loyalty now lay with her, the answer almost surely was yes.

Crutchfield was the one who patched Thurman up after his multiple injuries escaping from Jessie's apartment. One of those injuries was a nightstick to the forehead. Jessie had landed the vicious blow to the head with it, in the exact spot where that bandage now rested. Was the wound worse than it looked? It seemed that Crutchfield thought so.

Before Jessie knew what to do with the information, Thurman was on her, swinging the knife down at the right side of her body. She twisted away from him and felt the blade slice down her back behind her right shoulder, mowing through her flesh.

She heard a scream, certain it was her own. It took a second for her to process that it was actually the girl in the chair, who had finally managed to spit out the rag. It surprised Thurman too and he turned to look at her in shock. He went over to her, retrieved and replaced the rag in her mouth, then turned his attention back to Jessie.

The brief reprieve had given Jessie the time she needed to come up with an idea. It was simple and stupid and unlikely to work. But it was all she had.

170

She waited until her father lumbered toward her again, making sure not to move until he was too close to back away. Then, with all the strength she could muster, she tugged down on the bungee cords with her tied-up wrists and used the rebounding momentum to lift her legs high in the air. She extended them out in one quick, violent kicking motion.

The heel of her right shoe made perfect contact with the bandage on Thurman's forehead. She heard what she thought was a cracking sound as he stumbled backward, howling in pain. He bent over, trying to stem the sudden flow of blood spewing out around the bandage with one hand, while still holding the knife with the other.

When he looked back up at her, blood was streaming down the entire right side of his face, pouring into his eye. He wiped it away sloppily as he came at her, still moaning loudly. His already unsteady, shuffling gait was even clumsier as he bore down on her, his eyes blinking in a mix of pain and seeming confusion.

Behind him, the girl suddenly rocked back in the chair she was tied to and then violently flung herself forward, chair and all. Her body slammed into Xander's back as he moved away from her, knocking him off balance. He stumbled and dropped to the ground, landing on his knees in front of Jessie

He was clearly disoriented, but not so much that he couldn't raise the knife above his head, his unfocused eyes trained on the daughter directly before him.

As he did so, Jessie leapt up again, ignoring the crack she felt that probably indicated she'd broken her left wrist. Xander swung down, the blade slicing along the outer edge of Jessie's left calf as she clamped her legs around his neck.

With her legs resting on his shoulders, Jessie slammed her knees together hard, smashing her father's head between them. Before he processed what was happening, she did it again, and then a third time. Each time, she heard a gratifying thwack as the hard bones of her inner knees collided with her father's temples.

That didn't stop him from swinging at her. He jabbed at the knees that were the source of his agony. But because Jessie kept moving them back and forth, he only got in a few clean blows. Finally, one wild swing dug deep into her right thigh, embedding there.

Despite the searing anguish she felt in her leg, Jessie didn't stop beating her legs in and out. The force of the movement ripped the handle of the blade from Xander's hand. Jessie watched, almost as an observer, as her knees continued to box her father's skull, the butcher knife quivering as it protruded from her flesh.

Xander seemed bewildered now, his eyes unfocused, his breathing labored. He slumped forward slightly, held mostly upright by Jessie's legs. With his neck now squarely between her thighs, she compressed them together, using all her remaining strength to squeeze off his windpipe and choke every last bit of air out of him.

It seemed to be working, as his eyes bulged wide as he gasped for breath he couldn't find. And still she squeezed, even as it felt like the cord above her might tear her hands from her wrists.

Xander's eyes fluttered closed and his weight slumped completely forward into Jessie. She pulled her thighs apart and let him collapse to the ground face first. Her feet slammed hard against the floor, like heavy dumbbells being dropped. But knowing fatigue and unrelenting physical anguish would take over any second, she didn't allow herself even a moment to recover.

Bracing her left leg with the bloated knee on the floor, she raised her right leg, the one with the butcher knife still protruding from it, high in the air. Then she brought it down, her right foot slamming solidly into the back Xander's head, smashing his face into the floor.

She heard a dull, almost inaudible moan. The sound only infuriated her and she raised her leg again and once more brought it down hard, connecting in the same spot. She did it a third time and saw that the impact made the knife slide out of her thigh and tumble across the floor, where it rested beside the girl, still strapped to the chair, looking up at her.

Jessie returned her attention to her father and focused her concentration on the bloody spot on the back of his head, almost like an "X" on a treasure map. She lifted her leg once more, knowing that she only had the strength left for this final stomp. With every last bit of force she could muster, she brought her leg down. The heel of her foot hit solidly and she heard a satisfyingly sickening crack as a chunk of his skull splintered open.

CHAPTER THIRTY THREE

She was done.

Without even the energy to slide her foot off the back of Xander's head, Jessie slumped down, no longer aware or even interested in whether her arms were attached to her body. She breathed in slow, labored heaves. She could hear the blood dripping from various places on her body and splattering softy on the floor. Her eyes drifted lazily around the room as she flirted with unconsciousness.

They eventually settled on the girl in the chair, resting on its side on the floor. She was inching slowly toward the knife, which had landed near her. As she moved, the only sound in the room beside the continuous splatter of Jessie's blood was the scraping of the wooden chair as the girl moved. She scooted over until she was able to grip it with her right hand and angle the blade back toward her wrists. She began to saw back and forth at the duct tape.

It was a slow process and she cut into her own wrist as often as she cut the tape. Jessie heard her muffled cries through the rag each time she nicked herself especially hard. Eventually, she had snipped through enough of the tape that she was able to extricate her hand. She moved on to her left wrist, which came loose much quicker now that she had the full use of her right hand. After that, she pulled out the rag and looked up at Jessie.

"It's going to be all right, Junebug," she said reassuringly.

Jessie chuckled despite the pain. Of course, the girl had no idea what her real name was. She'd only ever heard Xander call her Junebug. So that's what she called her too.

The girl interpreted the laugh as a sign that Jessie was losing it, which wasn't far off. As quickly as she could, the girl cut her legs free and, with much effort, got to her feet. She shuffled over to Jessie, carefully avoiding the body of the man who'd tortured her and killed her family. Despite the blood oozing liberally from his head, she gave him a wide berth.

When she got close to Jessie, she wrapped an arm around her to help support her weight as she cut the cord attached to her left arm. Jessie slumped down hard and the girl had to adjust her position to hold her up. Then she cut the second cord and Jessie collapsed into her arms.

The girl had been expecting it and caught her before easing her gently to the ground. Jessie smiled up at the girl with the concerned look on her face.

Free of the restraints and the gag, she looked surprisingly composed, all things considered. Without the mask of fear contorting her face, Jessie pegged her age as about seventeen. Her sandy-blonde, shoulder-length hair clung sweatily to her neck. Her green eyes, puffy and red from crying, exuded intelligence.

"My name is Jessie," she mumbled, not sure if the words she tried to form were actually coherent.

"Hi, Jessie," the girl said, confirming they were. "I'm Hannah. I hear sirens outside. I'm going to get help. I promise I'll be right back."

Jessie nodded as the girl staggered off to the front of the house. After she was gone, Jessie managed to roll over from her side onto her back. She looked up at the body of the other woman, likely Hannah's mother, still dangling lifelessly above her. Somewhere off beyond the couch was the girl's father.

Rolling her head to the left, Jessie looked at Xander Thurman. His head was on its side so she could see his face. It was drenched in blood, as the wound on his forehead was still seeping. His eyes were open, though the left was so encased in blood she couldn't really see it.

But the right was mostly clear. And as she lay on the ground, waiting for help to arrive, Jessie stared at the green eye of the man who'd tried to kill her, her own father. She couldn't help but admit, as she drifted off into oblivion, that it really was like looking in a mirror.

CHAPTER THIRTY FOUR

Jessie was freezing.

It took her several seconds to realize that was because she was in a thin hospital gown with no sheets covering her in a chilly room and ice-cold oxygen blasting from a mask on her cracked, parched mouth.

She wanted desperately to ask for a blanket or at least an ice chip. But neither her mouth nor her body was reacting to her brain's instructions. Finally, after what felt like an eternity, she managed to do the one thing within her power: she groaned.

She couldn't open her eyes but heard shuffling nearby. Soon a voice she didn't recognize, likely a nurse, spoke to her soothingly.

"Ms. Hunt, you are at California Hospital Medical Center in downtown Los Angeles. I'm Joanie, your nurse. You were attacked and suffered several serious injuries. But the important thing to know is that you're going to be all right. You've been in surgery for the last several hours. Once you're stabilized, we'll move you out of the ICU. One of your colleagues will be in later to walk you through what happened to you. But for now, you need to rest."

"Ahhss," Jessie managed to moan.

"If you're asking for ice chips, we need to hold off on that until the doctor gives the all clear. I know you're uncomfortable. I'm going to rub some petroleum jelly on your lips, which may help a little. I'm also going to put a sheet over you in case you're cold. You have goose bumps. If you don't want that, make some kind of noise. If you don't say anything, I'll assume you're okay with it."

Jessie remained silent. Soon she felt the chill dissipate slightly, which she assumed was due to a sheet, though she never actually felt it on her skin. She did feel the Vaseline being rubbed on her lips, which offered a bit of relief.

She thought about trying to say thank you, but somewhere between the thought and the words, she slipped back into sleep.

*

This time, when she woke up, Jessie was actually capable of opening her eyes.

As she looked around the room, she was able to immediately tell that she was out of the ICU and in a regular room. For one thing, it was much quieter. Instead of dozens of beeps and voices, she heard only one machine beeping occasionally.

The lights were off and the shades were pulled. But the bright sun leaking through at the edges told her it was the middle of the day.

Which day though?

She glanced over at the two small, uncomfortable-looking chairs in the corner of the room. Both were occupied by sleeping people. One was Agent Dolan, who snored softly. In the other chair was Kat Gentry. If she was here, that meant she'd come from Europe, which suggested Jessie had been out for quite a while.

She saw movement out of the corner of her eye. A doctor was coming in. He must have noticed she'd woken up. Seeing Kat and Dolan asleep in the chairs, he closed the door quietly after entering and walked over without a sound. With his baby face and shaggy brown hair, he looked far too young be a doctor, though Jessie suspected he was probably older than she was.

"Hi," he whispered when he was right next to her. "I'm Dr. Riggs. You must be Jessie."

She nodded, not sure how effective her voice would be after this long without speaking.

"I'm sure you have a lot of questions," he said. "I can't answer all of them. But I can tell you how you're doing medically. Do you think you're up for that?"

She nodded again.

"Okay. The short version is that you don't have any permanent damage, though you will be moving slowly for a while. The knife wound to the right side of your back required thirty-seven stitches. You'll have limited mobility in that area for a while and will need extensive physical therapy. The wound to your right thigh was especially traumatic and will take quite some time to heal. And, of course, you're going to have a number of additional scars. Considering you were stabbed or cut over two dozen times and lost a lot of blood, I'd say you came out of the whole thing pretty well. You also have a cracked rib, a fractured left wrist, a strained right

176

ACL, and a concussion to go with a pretty sizable knot on your head. As you can imagine with that being the short version, the long version will take some time. But we can save that for later."

Jessie took a moment to let everything he'd said settle in. Considering that she wasn't sure she'd ever wake up when she drifted off in that mansion, she considered herself lucky.

"Murph?" she managed to croak. She braced herself for the answer.

Dr. Riggs looked perplexed.

"I'm not sure what that means," he said.

"She asking about the status of Marshal Murphy," Dolan said sleepily. His eyes remained closed.

"Oh yes, Patrick Murphy, the marshal who was hit by the car. He's actually in another surgery now. Both his legs were broken in the collision and then he fractured his clavicle when he hit the ground. He should eventually make a full recovery but it's going to take a while—easily six months."

Jessie nodded. It could have been far worse. It occurred to her that until this moment, she hadn't known the full name of the man who'd risked his life for her. The same was true for another man who'd sacrificed his.

"What about Emerson?" she asked, knowing the answer already.

The doctor looked confused, which made sense. He would only know about patients who needed treatment, not people who came to the hospital already dead. Dolan, with his eyes now open, sat fully upright. He shook his head.

"The service will be this weekend," he said quietly. "I'll FaceTime it if you can't go."

"She won't be able to attend, I'm afraid," Dr. Riggs said, picking up on the nature of the situation.

Jessie nodded, then thought of another question.

"And the girl—Hannah?"

Riggs clearly knew who she was talking about.

"Hannah Dorsey escaped with very little in the way of injuries. Lots of bruising. Her right wrist was pretty nicked up. But she said she did that herself when she was cutting off the tape. Her long-term issues are more likely to be psychological, as neither of her parents survived."

"I'll fill you in more on that later," Dolan said in a tone that suggested the conversation ought to be confidential. Beside him, Kat stirred, then opened her own eyes lazily.

"Sorry to wake you, princess," Jessie said hoarsely.

Kat's eyes opened wide and she hopped out of her chair and rushed over to the bedside.

"Gentle," Dr. Riggs warned her.

Kat stopped short of hugging her but smiled broadly.

"I can't leave you alone for a second, can I?" she said.

"Apparently not," Jessie allowed.

"I'll leave you all for a bit," Dr. Riggs interjected. "We can discuss your situation in more detail later. But for now, the one rule is: take it easy."

"Yes sir," Jessie said. She had every intention of following the rule.

Once he left, Jessie returned her attention to Kat.

"When did you get back?"

"About six hours ago. Your boy Hernandez gave me a call. I told the Interpol agent who didn't realize I knew he was watching me that he was off the hook and I caught the next flight back. I figured you might need a roommate slash nursemaid for a little while, until you're all better. Are you still considered a protectee of the Marshal Service?"

"I don't know. I'm kind of out of the loop," she said, turning to Dolan. "Am I?"

Technically yes," he said. "Corcoran says that as long as Crutchfield is out there, you're at risk."

Jessie debated how forthcoming to be and decided there wasn't much downside anymore.

"Yeah, about that. I didn't mention this earlier but Crutchfield was at the Jerebko house when I showed up to question them. He could have gotten the jump on me, which would have been his second opportunity to kill me in as many days. Instead, he showed me where exactly on the forehead Thurman was physically vulnerable. That was *after* warning me that Thurman might come after me at the safe house."

Dolan's mouth dropped open. Jessie waited for him to recover before continuing.

"Bolton Crutchfield may not be done messing with me. I think he views himself as a cat and me as the ball of yarn he likes batting around. But I feel pretty confident that he doesn't want to kill me."

"Are you willing to stake your life on that?" Dolan asked skeptically.

"I'm willing to get back to leading my life. I can't spend every moment looking over my shoulder. I want to be done with that. And with my father dead, I should be able to finally do that."

Neither Dolan nor Kat responded to that. Suddenly Jessie felt less confident.

"He is dead, isn't he?"

Dolan seemed to realize his silence had caused unexpected anxiety.

"Yes," he assured her quickly. "He is very much dead. In fact, Decker will probably have a few questions for you about that."

"What do you mean?"

"It's just that he's not only dead, he's 'windpipe-crushed, skull cracked open, brains oozing out' dead. There's a view among some that you used… unnecessary force."

"Unnecessary force?" Jessie repeated, her voice cracking in fury. "I was tied up and being slowly filleted. I got a momentary advantage and used it. I had to make sure he was no longer a threat. Should I have just tried to kick him in the balls and hoped for the best?"

"Calm down, Hunt," Dolan said softly. "I'm not questioning you. And I don't think Decker is either. I just think some of the bureaucrats looked at the nature of his injuries and raised concerns. They don't really appreciate the context."

"So am I in trouble?"

"No. I seriously doubt the civilian profiler who singlehandedly took down a serial killer who'd been on the loose for two decades and who is currently hospitalized is in any long-term trouble. But you may have to make a visit or two to the shrink to discuss your inner demons; you know, the ones that led you to split open your daddy's head like a melon."

"Like you should be talking about inner demons," she pointed out.

"Actually, Hunt, if anyone should be able to speak to them, it's me," he said. "You've seen how I deal with what happened to my family. I think we both can agree it's not the healthiest way handle

179

to handle past trauma. And it leads for a lonely life. There's a reason I work sixteen hours a day. I don't have anything to go home to. I'd hate for you to end up like that, Hunt; lonely and angry with double bourbons as your only refuge from the pain."

Jessie wasn't sure how to respond to that. She saw that Kat was equally uncomfortable with the roguish FBI agent's sudden earnestness. Finally, deciding this wasn't the time to focus on how she was processing her father's death, she determined the best course was to change the subject entirely.

"Yeah, well. Maybe you should be working less than sixteen hours because you got it wrong. I didn't take down Thurman single-handedly. If it hadn't been for that Hannah girl, I'd be dead right now. She really stepped up when it mattered."

Dolan smiled, happy to let the sincere moment pass as well.

"Speaking of the girl, that's what I wanted to fill you in on after the doctor left. We learned a little more about her."

"Yeah," Jessie remembered. "Thurman said her family didn't live there—that he brought them in from another neighborhood entirely. Do we know what that's about?"

Dolan glanced over at Kat hesitantly.

"Okay to speak freely in front of your pal here?" he asked.

"Absolutely," Jessie guaranteed him. "She's in the circle of trust."

"I'm flattered," Kat said with a smirk, though she was blushing at the compliment.

"Okay," Dolan continued. "We're pretty sure we know the reason your father specifically brought them in. As you know, he had the whole scenario planned out—to kill the parents and then you and have Hannah watch the whole thing."

"Right, he said as much."

"Yes," Dolan said, now choosing his words more slowly and carefully. "We believe he was repeating the cycle."

"What cycle?" Jessie asked. "Of making a young girl watch, tied up in a chair, as people are murdered in front of her?"

"Not just any people, Hunt. We interviewed Hannah earlier. Apparently, the Dorseys adopted her when she was a baby. On a hunch, I had the doctors do a blood test on her. And she was a match."

"A match for who?" Jessie asked, her stomach already tightening in apprehension.

180

"For two people: her father, Xander Thurman. And you, Jessie. Hannah is your half-sister."

NOW AVAILABLE!

THE PERFECT LIE
(A Jessie Hunt Psychological Suspense Thriller—Book Five)

"A masterpiece of thriller and mystery. Blake Pierce did a magnificent job developing characters with a psychological side so well described that we feel inside their minds, follow their fears and cheer for their success. Full of twists, this book will keep you awake until the turn of the last page."
--Books and Movie Reviews, Roberto Mattos (re Once Gone)

THE PERFECT LIE is book #5 in a new psychological suspense series by bestselling author Blake Pierce, whose #1 bestseller Once Gone (a free download) has over 1,000 five-star reviews.

When a gorgeous, popular gym trainer is found murdered in a wealthy suburban town, criminal profiler and FBI agent Jessie Hunt, 29, is called in to find out who killed her. Yet the twisted secrets that this affair-ridden town holds is unlike anything she has encountered before.

Who was this woman sleeping with? How many marriages did she shatter?

And why did they want her dead?

A fast-paced psychological suspense thriller with unforgettable characters and heart-pounding suspense, THE PERFECT LIE is book #5 in a riveting new series that will leave you turning pages late into the night.

Book #6 in the Jessie Hunt series will be available soon

.

Did you know that I've written multiple novels in the mystery genre? If you haven't read all my series, download a series starter!

Blake Pierce

Blake Pierce is author of the bestselling RILEY PAGE mystery series, which includes fifteen books (and counting). Blake Pierce is also the author of the MACKENZIE WHITE mystery series, comprising thirteen books (and counting); of the AVERY BLACK mystery series, comprising six books; of the KERI LOCKE mystery series, comprising five books; of the MAKING OF RILEY PAIGE mystery series, comprising five books (and counting); of the KATE WISE mystery series, comprising six books (and counting); of the CHLOE FINE psychological suspense mystery, comprising six books (and counting); and of the JESSE HUNT psychological suspense thriller series, comprising five books (and counting).

An avid reader and lifelong fan of the mystery and thriller genres, Blake loves to hear from you, so please feel free to visit www.blakepierceauthor.com to learn more and stay in touch.

BOOKS BY BLAKE PIERCE

A JESSIE HUNT PSYCHOLOGICAL SUSPENSE SERIES
THE PERFECT WIFE (Book #1)
THE PERFECT BLOCK (Book #2)
THE PERFECT HOUSE (Book #3)
THE PERFECT SMILE (Book #4)
THE PERFECT LIE (Book #5)

CHLOE FINE PSYCHOLOGICAL SUSPENSE SERIES
NEXT DOOR (Book #1)
A NEIGHBOR'S LIE (Book #2)
CUL DE SAC (Book #3)
SILENT NEIGHBOR (Book #4)
HOMECOMING (Book #5)
TINTED WINDOWS (Book #6)

KATE WISE MYSTERY SERIES
IF SHE KNEW (Book #1)
IF SHE SAW (Book #2)
IF SHE RAN (Book #3)
IF SHE HID (Book #4)
IF SHE FLED (Book #5)
IF SHE FEARED (Book #6)

THE MAKING OF RILEY PAIGE SERIES
WATCHING (Book #1)
WAITING (Book #2)
LURING (Book #3)
TAKING (Book #4)
STALKING (Book #5)

RILEY PAIGE MYSTERY SERIES
ONCE GONE (Book #1)
ONCE TAKEN (Book #2)
ONCE CRAVED (Book #3)
ONCE LURED (Book #4)
ONCE HUNTED (Book #5)
ONCE PINED (Book #6)
ONCE FORSAKEN (Book #7)
ONCE COLD (Book #8)
ONCE STALKED (Book #9)
ONCE LOST (Book #10)
ONCE BURIED (Book #11)